DOUBLE-FISTED IRON

"Cover me, Chaw!" Rawley barked.

The grizzled ex-deputy shouldered his carbine and laid down a steady stream of hot lead in the direction of the outlaws. Rawley lit out into the tall grass.

Working his way down the draw, he made it to a few yards from the gun-totin' rustlers. Rawley put his carbine in his left hand and drew his Colt with his right. "Hold there, you two!"

The raiders did not hesitate a second, turned and leveled on Rawley. But he shot first and fast, his pistol bucking with each bullet as the hot lead cut down the hooded desperadoes.

They fell like bags of grain from a supply wagon onto the blood-soaked ground.

POWELL'S ARMY
BY TERENCE DUNCAN

#1: UNCHAINED LIGHTNING   (1994, $2.50)

Thundering out of the past, a trio of deadly enforcers dispenses its own brand of frontier justice throughout the untamed American West! Two men and one woman, they are the U.S. Army's most lethal secret weapon—they are POWELL'S ARMY!

#2: APACHE RAIDERS   (2073, $2.50)

The disappearance of seventeen Apache maidens brings tribal unrest to the violent breaking point. To prevent an explosion of bloodshed, Powell's Army races through a nightmare world south of the border—and into the deadly clutches of a vicious band of Mexican flesh merchants!

#3: MUSTANG WARRIORS   (2171, $2.50)

Someone is selling cavalry guns and horses to the Comanche—and that spells trouble for the bluecoats' campaign against Chief Quanah Parker's bloodthirsty Kwahadi warriors. But Powell's Army are no strangers to trouble. When the showdown comes, they'll be ready—and someone is going to die!

#4: ROBBERS ROOST   (2285, $2.50)

After hijacking an army payroll wagon and killing the troopers riding guard, Three-Fingered Jack and his gang high-tail it into Virginia City to spend their ill-gotten gains. But Powell's Army plans to apprehend the murderous hardcases before the local vigilantes do—to make sure that Jack and his slimy band stretch hemp the legal way!

TEXAS DRAWDOWN

PATRICK ANDREWS

ZEBRA BOOKS
KENSINGTON PUBLISHING CORP.

This book is dedicated to my sister

MICHAELA ANDREWS

ZEBRA BOOKS

are published by

Kensington Publishing Corp.
475 Park Avenue South
New York, NY 10016

First printing: May, 1991

Printed in the United States of America

Chapter 1

The two horsemen rode easily and slowly across the
flat west Texas landscape. They had come a long way
and still had a great distance to go, so neither one saw
the sense in wearing out the animals at that particular
stage of their difficult journey. They slouched noticeably in the saddle, fighting to stay awake to keep their
mounts from wandering off the slightly northwest
course they followed across the trackless prairie.

The taller one was also the younger. Broad-
shouldered with coal-black hair and bright green eyes,
Rawley Pierson was in his early thirties. Slim but with
a sinewy muscularity, he had an easy grin and a rugged
face that the ladies found irresistible. But that grin
could turn to a scowl when he was angered. Rawley's
manner of dress showed he preferred to spend most of
his time in town rather than out on the range. The
trousers and shirt were more for the street than the
open country. But the wide-brimmed sombrero and
chaps he wore also gave evidence he could be an
outdoorsman when he had to.

The Colt in the holster tied down low on his right
thigh and the Winchester in his saddle-boot also
exhibited a side of his makeup that would make most

sensible folks think twice before seriously riling Rawley Pierson. He was good enough with those irons to be paid for his services.

Rawley's traveling companion was a lot older. Chaw Stevens had served with Hood's Texans of the Confederate Army from start to finish in that Southern rebellion over twenty years before. Chaw was forty-five, looked sixty-five, and was bewhiskered and generally bad-tempered. He wore a battered old hat with its wide brim turned up at the front. His careless choice of dress showed in a faded, worn shirt with the elbows completely worn out. An ancient pair of buckskin trousers was stuffed into scuffed high-top boots that sported badly worn heels.

The bulge of chewing tobacco in his cheek showed how he'd earned his moniker. Short and wiry, he was a bandy-legged little man who looked at life through squinting eyes as if staring into a hot desert sun. Excitable and quick to act, he could get into more trouble than was natural for a codger his age. Most of those difficulties came about when he voiced his mostly contrary opinions.

But today Chaw was in a good mood.

"Sumbitch!" he exclaimed with a cackle. "It do feel good to get rid o' them tin stars."

"That's about the hundredth time you said that since we left Benton," Rawley said, coming out of a doze at the sound of his old friend's voice.

"Well, by God, I'll prob'ly say it a hunnerd more times afore we get up to Delbert's place," Chaw told him.

Rawley shook his head. "I dunno."

"What the hell's the matter with you? After two years as the town law you think you'd be glad to have a change," Chaw said. "Particular when the folks you put your butt on the line for don't appreciate the risks you

6

take. Anyhow, you was ready to change. That's for sure."

Rawley shrugged. "Maybe."

"Maybe, my Aunt Bessie's tits!" Chaw exclaimed. "I could tell from the way you was always staring off in space that it was time to pull stakes and go."

"I ain't sure if going back to cow-punching is that good an idea," Rawley said. "That ain't real easy work."

"You been in town too long," Chaw retorted. "Once you're out from under a town job and are out there on that range, you'll get them ol' stirrings again. You can trust me on that. Working for a ranch ain't easy, but you got more freedom."

"Maybe."

"I've knowed you since you was a tad, Rawley Pierson," Chaw said. "When I come back from the war you'd been out on your pa's ranch all your life. That's your beginnings and they can't be denied."

"Maybe."

"And we're gonna have our own herd to drive north in a coupla more years if we play our cards right. That's what this damn trip is all about." Chaw spat out the stale tobacco in his mouth. He reached inside his leather vest and pulled out a plug. He took a bite and shoved the remnant back in its resting place. "It ain't natural for some men to live in a town. Besides, if we kept packing them stars we'd end up in boot hill. You can't beat 'em all."

"I reckon not." Rawley stood in his stirrups and stretched away some of the kinks before sitting down again in the saddle. "I got to admit I was getting edgy. Someday one or both of us would've caught it from a feller a little faster."

"My idea was the best," Chaw said. "Get outta all this law business and back to what we really are—

7

cattlemen. We got a few dollars saved. Once we're back in practice at ranching, we can get that outfit of our own. And ol' Delbert's place up there in New Mexico is a mighty good location to start up again and get that god-awful town stink outta our noses."

Delbert Wayland was an old friend of the pair who had a nice spread just short of the Colorado line. A Texan by birth, he'd known Rawley and Chaw since boyhood. When he'd found out from a passing friend that the pair were in Benton, Texas, he'd sent off a letter offering them jobs for the coming roundup. It took the missive three months to find Rawley and Chaw. But tired of being sheriff and deputy, they'd decided to take him up on the offer for at least one seasonal drive. Then their plans were to strike out on their own, and get a herd to run and a place they'd stay on for the rest of their lives.

A distant gunshot sounded over the horizon. Both men looked in that direction.

"Could be a hunter," Rawley said.

"Yeah? Then let's be careful his game ain't heading this way or we'll catch a stray slug as sure as shit stinks," Chaw said. "An excited hunter is a right careless sumbitch at times."

Another shot followed. Then another. Within moments an entire fusillade sounded.

"Let's see what's going on," Rawley said, spurring his horse.

"Hold up!" Chaw said. "We got to keep on straight to reach Delbert's place. Hell, we ain't got time for no damn wandering around." But he followed his younger friend.

They cantered in the direction of the shooting until they topped a rise. Looking down, they could see the source of the noise. Two riders, going desperately fast, were being chased by at least a dozen others who were blasting at them in furious abandon.

"Hey!" Chaw exclaimed. "Them fellers doing the chasing is wearing hoods."

"Folks that hide their faces are generally up to no good," Rawley said.

"They might be vigilantes," Chaw suggested.

"Yeah," Rawley remarked. "And them two being chased might be a coupla rustlers too."

"Is that something we're gonna have to decide here real quick?" Chaw asked.

"Yeah. And I vote that them masked jaspers ain't vigilantes," Rawley said, making up his mind.

Chaw looked over at him. "You know, most folks who were strangers on an unknown range wouldn't want to get tangled up in a situation like that."

"That's right," Rawley agreed. "Particular when they didn't know what it was all about."

"But we ain't most folks, are we?" Chaw asked, grinning.

"We never was, pardner," Rawley said.

"Whose side did you say we're on?"

"Them two getting chased," Rawley answered. "They're outnumbered and they ain't wearing masks. Anyhow, ain't that our style?"

"Damn right!"

They kicked their horses' flanks and galloped fast toward the traveling melee. By making a diagonal cut that took them behind a stand of cottonwoods, they were able to stay out of sight until they burst on the scene almost directly behind the hooded pursuers. Now they pulled their pistols and cut loose, the salvos zipping across the prairie at the masked men.

One of the horsemen twisted in his saddle, his gun arm going limp. Surprised and shocked, he pulled away from the chase. Rawley and Chaw closed in, pumping ill-aimed shots that still managed to slap into

9

the crowd of eleven men ahead of them. Another rider suddenly went forward as a slug struck him between the shoulder blades. He tried to hang on, but slipped out of the saddle and hit the deep grass, bouncing twice before rolling to a halt.

Now the two men being chased noted they were getting help. Wanting to give their unknown rescuers a better chance, they cut sharply inward, making the route shorter. Rawley and Chaw continued firing, dumping another of the riders. When the others finally noticed the pair closing in on them, their surprise caused them to veer away. They kept right on going until they had galloped over the horizon out of sight.

Up ahead, the men who had been human prey only moments before reined up. They waited for their rescuers to join them. One was a middle-aged man with a craggy, sweat-soaked face. He reached out to offer his hand when Rawley rode up.

"I don't know who the hell you are, mister. But I'm obliged as all hell to you."

"Damn right," his companion said. "I plain didn't think we was gonna make it."

Chaw observed the formalities by introducing himself and Rawley. "I'm Chaw Stevens and this is my pard Rawley Pierson."

"Jim Pauley," one said.

"I'm Duane Wheeler."

"I don't want to appear nosey," Rawley said. "But I'm a mite curious how two fellers could get a dozen others so damn mad at 'em."

Pauley laughed. "Hell, mister. All you got to do to get shot at around these parts is be a cowpuncher."

Rawley looked at Chaw and grinned. "Still think it's better'n being a star-packer?"

"In most parts it is, goddamnit!" Chaw snapped.

"We're off the Circle H Bar," Wheeler said.

10

"It's owned by the Hawkins folks," Pauley added. He thought there might be a chance that the two strangers had helped them because they knew the family they worked for. "You friends o' theirs?"

"Nope," Rawley said. "We just got a natural dislike for gunslingers that hide their faces."

Wheeler laughed. "You just like to jump in where the odds is against you, huh? Well, mister, that was all right with me."

Pauley noticed their gear. "You boys is traveling, ain't you? Why'nt you come on over to the ranch and let us intr'duce you to Hawkins. He'll prob'ly give you a good hot meal for helping out."

"That's the best offer I've heard today," Rawley said, tired of eating trail grub.

"Lead on, boys," Chaw urged them.

The four riders showed some consideration for their tired horses by making the ride across the rolling land an easy one. But they instinctively kept their eyes on the horizon in case more dry-gulchers suddenly burst into view.

They managed to reach the ranch a half hour later, riding into the yard and up to the corral. All dismounted and tied their horses to the rail fence. The slamming of a door at the house caught their attention.

A gray-haired man, limping a bit, came out. He had a huge handle-bar mustache set under a large, hook nose. His wrinkled skin was as much from years spent in the outdoors as it was from advanced age.

"What the hell happened?" he asked.

"Howdy, Mister Hawkins," Wheeler said. "Me and Jim was tending the south herd and got jumped. If these two fellers hadn't lent a hand, we'd be two carcasses out on the prairie by now."

"Howdy," Hawkins said. "Zeb Hawkins."

"Rawley Pierson."

11

"Chaw Stevens."

"I give you my thanks," the ranch owner said.

"You're welcome," Rawley replied.

"They got two of 'em, Mister Hawkins," Wheeler said. "But we couldn't take time to go back and look at 'em."

"That's the trouble," Hawkins remarked. "They outnumber us so even if we get one or two, there ain't no chance of pulling them damn hoods off to see who they are."

"Have you tried trailing 'em back to their camp or hideout?" Chaw asked.

"Yeah. But all we've found is cold ashes and piles o' shit," Zeb Hawkins said. "They move around a lot so they can't be nailed down."

"Sounds like you got a real job ahead of you before you clear this mess up," Rawley said.

Hawkins snapped his eyes back to Wheeler. "What about the herd?"

"Stampeded, I reckon," Wheeler said. "We'll have to go out and round 'em up again."

"I could see somebody going to all that trouble to steal cattle," Hawkins said. "But why go through so damn much just to scatter 'em? Must be a joke."

"We buried four fellers on account o' them jokes," Pauley reminded him.

The door at the house slammed again. This time a decidedly pretty young woman came out. She wore a blue calico dress and had done up her light-brown hair in a bun.

Jim Pauley and Duane Wheeler took off their hats. "Howdy, Miss Nancy."

Nancy Hawkins nodded and smiled. "More trouble?"

"Yes, ma'am," Wheeler said. "But this time we got help."

12

Chaw looked at her with a mistrustful glare in his bachelor eyes. "I'm Chaw Stevens, ma'am. This here is Rawley Pierson."

Rawley smiled easily, subtly admiring her pretty face. "At your service," he said politely.

"This is my daughter," Hawkins said. "And don't let that dress fool you. She can ride, rope, and herd with the best of 'em. And it's a damn good thing too. I ain't been able to keep much of a crew."

"None of the ranchers on the Diablos Range has," Nancy added.

"I'm kinda confused," Rawley said. "You talked like nobody rustled your cattle, but only scattered 'em."

"After shooting any careless cowboy nearby," Duane Wheeler said.

"Why don't we all go into the house and I'll explain what's going on to you," Hawkins said. "By the way, are you two fellers looking for a job?"

"We already got one," Chaw quickly interjected. "Up in New Mexico. That's where we're a-headed."

"Come on in the house anyway," Hawkins said. "The least we can do is take the wrinkles outta your bellies with some good food and give you few swallows of whiskey to cut the trail dust."

Nancy led the way back as Rawley, Chaw, and Hawkins followed.

Chapter 2

The ranch house showed Nancy Hawkins's strong influence. The furniture, though not fancy or expensive, was well arranged and covered with doilies. Family portraits were lined neatly along the top of the fireplace.

"Make yourselves to home, boys," Hawkins said. "Don't be afeared to use the furniture."

He went to a cabinet holding a bottle of whiskey and glasses. Nancy settled onto a settee at the side of the room, not so much to keep out of the way as to be able to see what was going on.

Chaw walked over to the sofa and gently sat down, letting his trail-weary butt relax into the softness of the overstuffed piece of furniture. He emitted a long sigh. "Now this is right nice, I must say!"

Rawley, feeling the need for some stretching after sitting in the saddle so long, walked over to the mantel and looked at the pictures.

One, an old-fashioned tintype, showed a stern-looking young man sitting beside an unsmiling girl who appeared to be in her late teens. Hawkins, pouring out some tumblers of whiskey, noted Rawley studying the double portrait. "That's my first wife," he said.

"Is that young feller with her you?" Rawley asked.

Hawkins grinned as he handed a glass of liquor to a grateful Chaw. "Sure is. I was nineteen at the time. We had that pitcher took right afore we left Kentucky." He walked over and gave Rawley his drink. "She didn't last long out here. It was terrible hard for a woman in those days." He went back to his liquor cabinet and fixed his own libation.

Nancy, who had been doing her best to watch the handsome Rawley without being obvious about it, said, "He married my mother ten years later."

"I lost her too," Hawkins said. He took a deep breath. "I need a drink bad."

Rawley raised his glass. "Here's to fast horses."

"And fat cattle," Chaw added.

They drank and Hawkins said, "Mister Stevens is definitely a cowman."

"That I am," Chaw agreed. "Right down to my spurs."

Rawley took a swallow of the liquor. "You were gonna tell us about your troubles, Mister Hawkins?"

"You mean like having some masked sonofabitches trying to run me outta business and not being able to keep a full crew hired on?" Hawkins asked. "Is them the troubles you mean?"

Rawley smiled. "Not unless you got more'n that."

"I'll let Nancy explain it, Mister Pierson," Hawkins said. "I just get upset when I start talking 'bout what's going on. There ain't no sense to it a-tall."

"All the ranchers here on the Diablos Range are being harassed," Nancy began. "Naturally, we haven't the slightest idea who the raiders are because of those hoods. However, none of the cattle are stolen. They're just run off or scattered and left alone."

15

"That don't make a lick o' sense," Chaw said.

"I know it doesn't," Nancy said. "They don't attack the ranches themselves, just crews working out on the Diablos. And that means some cowhands have been murdered."

"Yeah," Rawley said. "We noticed that was what was about to happen to Jim Pauley and Duane Wheeler a bit ago."

"Who's doing it?" Chaw asked. He shrugged sheepishly. "I reckon that's a stupid question, ain't it? Particular since nobody can see their faces."

Hawkins was diplomatic. "Well, Chaw, I'd allow that if we knowed who it was they'd get took care of pronto. Or if we could find where they hang out between them cowardly raids."

"We can't even guess who the raiders might be, Mister Stevens," Nancy replied. "It's all a big mystery."

"Aw!" Hawkins exclaimed. "It don't make a lick o' sense!" He waved his glass around. "None of it!"

Further conversation was interrupted by a rap on the door. The two drovers, Jim Pauley and Duane Wheeler, stepped inside. "Begging your pardon, Mister Hawkins," Wheeler said. "But we're giving notice."

"C'mon, boys!" Hawkins said. "You can't leave me like this!"

"We're right sorry," Pauley chimed in. "But we're getting out while we're still in one piece. We been in range wars before, Mister Hawkins, but we knowed who to shoot back at."

"Yes, sir," Wheeler said. "And we had plenty o' good cowboys on our side to help out too."

"Damn, boys," Hawkins said weakly. "If you'd . . ." He paused. "Hell! Lemme pay you off." He left the living room and came back a few minutes later with some dollars. "I tally it up at thirty-five apiece since it

16

ain't roundup yet."

"That's fine, Mister Hawkins," Wheeler said.

Hawkins handed them the money, then shook hands. "I'm obliged you stayed as long as you did."

"Yes, sir," Wheeler said. "Adios, Mister Hawkins. Miss Hawkins. And to you two fellers."

"So long," Rawley said.

Hawkins's shoulders slumped as they left. "They was the last." He glanced up at Rawley and started to speak.

Chaw quickly said, "We got a job waiting for us in New Mexico. We been riding clear from Benton, Texas, to get to it."

"It'll be up to me, my boy, and my girl," Hawkins said.

"You have a son?" Rawley asked.

"Yeah," Hawkins answered. "He's out to the other side o' the spread."

"At any rate, are you offering us a job, Mister Hawkins?" Rawley asked.

"Yeah," Hawkins replied. "You'll get thirty a month and found." He took another drink. "I hate to admit it, but it ain't much to offer a feller to risk his life. But that's the best I can do right now. Naturally, I'll put forth a big bonus when . . ." The old rancher paused and shrugged. "I mean *if* we get the herd up to Kansas."

"You mean *when,* Papa," Nancy interjected.

"We'll take the jobs," Rawley said.

Chaw jumped up off the sofa. "Rawley! Goddamn it!"

"Watch your language, Chaw," Rawley said, indicating Nancy.

"I told you my daughter can rope and ride," Hawkins said. "I forgot to tell you she can cuss a blue streak when she's mad enough."

17

"Papa!" Nancy exclaimed, embarrassed.

"Are you serious about working for me, Mister Pierson?" Hawkins asked.

"Yes, sir. And I reckon you can call me Rawley since I'm on your payroll now."

Chaw sighed dejectedly. "And you can call me Chaw."

Hawkins grinned, his craggy face creased with happiness. "Boys, I really appreciate this. Maybe with your help we can pull outta this mess."

Another interruption to the conversation came from the sound of a horseman arriving at the front of the house. The door opened and a slim, young man walked in. Blond, with an arrogant look about him, he stood in the middle of the room with his arms crossed. "I passed Pauley and Wheeler on the road," he said sullenly. "Looks like we lost the last o' the crew."

"Don't worry, Tim," Hawkins said. "These two is taking their place."

Rawley gave the young man a friendly smile. "I'm Rawley Pierson. This is my pard Chaw Stevens."

Nancy said, "This is my brother Tim."

Tim was decidedly unfriendly. "And where'd you two drag in from?"

"Tim!" Nancy exclaimed. "That's no way to talk to new hands under the circumstances!"

"They saved Pauley and Wheeler's life when they was being chased by raiders," Hawkins said. "So you just simmer down, young man."

"Sure," Tim said. "I wouldn't want a coupla heroes mad at me." He walked through the living room. "My day's work is done. I'm going to town."

"You stay out of that Deep River Saloon," Nancy said. "And keep away from the owner, Ed Mac-Williams."

18

Tim turned around and laughed. "Big Ed is a swell feller and I like hanging around him. Particular when it's the only place a feller can go to relax around the Diablos." He winked at Nancy. "Anyhow, Big Ed thinks a lot o' you, sis. Maybe you oughta change your mind about him. He's a rich man."

Nancy's face reddened. "Big Ed MacWilliams is a tinhorn gambler and promises nothing but trouble for anyone who has anything to do with him."

"Your sister is right," Hawkins said.

"Pa," Tim said. "I do my work around here and earn my pay. Don't that make me a man?"

"It does," Hawkins admitted.

"Then I want to be treated like a man and be allowed to have a few drinks after a hard day's work," Tim said. "There ain't nothing else to do today, is there?"

"It's too late to round up the scattered herd," Hawkins said. "But we'll see to that first thing in the morning."

"Then I oughta be able to go to town for some relaxation and drinks then."

"I can't argue you on that, son," Hawkins said.

Tim quickly walked out of the living room and stomped up the stairs. Rawley watched him disappear, then turned to Chaw. "I reckon we might as well move into the bunkhouse."

"I reckon," Chaw said sullenly.

"We'll be having supper in 'bout an hour," Nancy said. "I'll give you a call."

"Thank you, Miss Nancy," Rawley said.

He led Chaw out of the house and over to their horses. After taking the animals to the corral and unsaddling them, they made sure they got a good feed out of the troughs inside the fenced barrier.

Carrying their gear, the pair of friends walked across

19

the ranch yard to the bunkhouse. They went inside and found a dozen unused bunks.

Rawley laughed. "Looks like we got a pretty good choice of where we're gonna sleep."

"Yeah," Chaw mumbled. "This is one outfit where there ain't no fights to be next to the stove in the winter or the windows in the summer."

Rawley picked a lower bunk and dropped his saddlebags and bedroll on it. "Now, Chaw, you're gonna feel mighty good 'bout yourself after we help these folks out."

"The hell if I will!" Chaw sputtered. "I'll feel like I do now—like a damn fool."

"Did you feel like a fool after helping out Pauley and Wheeler when them hooded bushwhackers was chasing them?" Rawley asked.

"No."

"Then it's the same thing as helping out the Hawkins," Rawley said.

"You got a way of twisting things around, Rawley," Chaw said. "I always come up with sensible ideas and work hard on bringing 'em around, and you spoil it all with your damn craziness."

Rawley untied his bedroll and spread it over the slats in the bunk. "You wanted us to give up being lawmen and get back to ranching. So we done it."

"I didn't mean here, goddamn it! Right in the middle of a war with masked desperadoes!" Chaw sputtered as he worked on his own bed. "I meant at Delbert's place in New Mexico."

"Delbert don't even know we're coming," Rawley said. "So he ain't gonna be mad if we don't show up."

"I don't want to talk about it no more," Chaw said. "We're here at a place where we're gonna get shot for thirty dollars a month and a bonus that we prob'ly won't ever see."

"Mister Hawkins is in trouble," Rawley said. "Think on that."

Chaw finished his chore, then settled down on his bunk. "I didn't say this wasn't the right thing to do. I was saying it was a dumb thing to do."

Rawley stretched out. "This ain't a bad bunk."

"Well, if you don't like it there's ten more in here to choose from," Chaw said.

Rawley laughed.

A few minutes later the partners heard Nancy Hawkins's voice calling them to supper across the ranch yard. The two new hands eagerly got up and went to the well at the back of the house. They found soap and towels waiting for them. Both washed up better than they normally would because of the young woman's presence.

When they went inside they could smell the fried potatoes, gravy, and steaks. Rawley looked at Chaw and winked.

Chaw frowned, whispering, "I never said the grub wouldn't be good."

Zeb Hawkins was already seated. They joined him, and Nancy sat down too. The old rancher bowed his head. "Lord," he said. "We thank you for what we're about to eat. Amen." Then he looked up. "Dig in, boys!"

The platter of well-done steaks made the rounds, followed by a bowl of boiled potatoes. This was followed by biscuits. Soon the only sound in the room was that of eating.

Rawley looked up and caught Nancy's eye. She smiled and looked away. Chaw stuck a forkful of steak in his mouth and chewed thoughtfully.

"A penny for your thoughts, Chaw," Hawkins said,

21

noting his pensive mood.

Chaw looked at him and swallowed. "I was just wondering what tomorrow would bring."

"There's only one thing for certain," Hawkins said. "There ain't been no easy days lately on the Circle H Bar."

Chapter 3

Big Ed MacWilliams sat tipped back in the chair on the porch of the Deep River Saloon. Big Ed was a large man with a thick neck and meaty shoulders. His expensive hat concealed his baldness. His jowls were close-shaven, but the heaviness of his beard was evident in the bluish tinge on his jaws.

One of his men, Shorty Clemens, stood beside him staring out at the waning activity on the main street of Duncan, Texas. "Weather's showing that spring is set in solid now, Boss." He was a small, thin man with a brutal, weather-beaten face. "Shouldn't be no more o' them cold north winds coming in over the Diablos Range." From the manner in which he spoke, it was obvious he was doing more than making a casual observance on the climate.

"Yeah," Big Ed said. "It's my fav'rite time o' year, Shorty."

Shorty laughed. "I bet."

"It's when the earth comes alive again after winter," Big Ed MacWilliams went on. He reached in his vest and pulled out a cigar, biting off the end. "It's nature's way of giving us a second chance." He spat out the piece of tobacco. "That's the way I look at it."

"Is that right, Boss? I figgered you looked at spring as the time the Texas cow herds would be coming through on their way up to Kansas," Shorty pointed out. "Among other things, that is. At least for this year."

"Don't get gabby," Big Ed said with a warning tone in his voice. Then his manner softened a bit. "But on the other hand, you could be right," the saloon owner added. He lit his cigar. "I got to admit I don't object none to them drovers spending an advance on their pay here in the Deep River."

The batwing doors swung open and Hannah O'Dell joined the two men. She was a hard-faced saloon woman who'd spent most of her life getting men drunk for her own profit and advantage. She smiled, but there was no pleasantness in her expression. "What the hell are you two up to out here?"

"Me and Shorty are just talking 'bout the weather," Big Ed said.

"I doubt that!" Hannah erupted into a short, harsh laugh. "You can't turn no Yankee dollars off with the weather."

Another of the Deep River Saloon's women, Rosalie Kinnon, stepped out. "I got to get some fresh air," she said. Like Hannah, she looked like a dance-hall girl, but with a better humor. Much younger, her face was rouged to entice customers to buy her the watered-down liquor kept just for that purpose behind the bar.

Big Ed looked up at her. "There ain't much going on tonight, is there?"

"There sure ain't," Rosalie complained. She was freckled with reddish-brown hair. Her face, though plain, was pleasant and friendly enough to coax a drink or trip upstairs from any lonely cowboy. "A girl can't make much money on evenings like this one."

24

"The drives is on their way," Shorty pointed out.

"It's about time," Rosalie said. "These winters drag on too damn long."

"See, Hannah?" Big Ed said, laughing. "Somebody else who appreciates nature like me and Shorty."

"You're all a bunch o' talkers," Hannah commented caustically.

Something caught Shorty's eye and he stepped out on the street for a better look. He hopped back up on the porch. "Well, gals, looks like work is coming this way even if it ain't necessarily for you two."

"What are you talking about?" Rosalie asked.

"Tim Hawkins is riding up the street," Shorty said.

"Is there a poker game inside?" Big Ed asked.

"If there ain't, I'll have one going directly," Shorty said, going into the interior of the saloon.

"Now you make Tim welcome," Big Ed said to Rosalie. "I think he kinda likes you, don't he?"

"He likes both of us," Rosalie said. "He just grabs the nearest one."

"Well, till the cowboys show up and I can afford to hire some more gals, it's just you and Hannah working. So make him feel welcome," Big Ed said.

"Don't we always," Hannah remarked.

Tim Hawkins rode up with an easy grin. He swung himself out of the saddle and hit the ground lightly. After looping the reins around the hitching rail, he stepped up on the porch, boldly eyeing the two women.

"Looking for a good time, Tim?" Hannah asked in a sultry voice.

"Maybe later," Tim replied. He nodded to Big Ed. "I gotta go to the bank."

Big Ed laughed. "Now that's gonna be bad news for the boys inside."

"Is there a game going?" Tim asked.

"Sure is," Big Ed said. He stood up and walked into

25

the saloon with Tim and the two women following.

Shorty Clemens, sitting at the poker table, waved over at Tim. "Hey, Tim Hawkins! Are you gonna give us a chance to get even?"

"Sure, boys, hang on till I get my money," Tim said.

He and Big Ed went into the office at the back of the building. The owner knelt down at a floor safe and worked the combination. Within moments he had withdrawn a stack of bills. "There's seven hundred dollars here," he said.

Tim laughed. "I didn't know there was that much."

"You get so damn drunk you forget," Big Ed said, chuckling. "Good thing you got a friend like me."

"I reckon," Tim agreed, taking the money. "I appreciate you holding onto this for me, Big Ed. If my pa found out I had it, he'd make me put it into the ranch before I could really build it into something. He's got to promise his hands a big bonus once the herd's in Kansas as it is."

"A man with poker-playing talent like you has got to get his money by what he does best," Big Ed advised him. "Anyhow, you'll be able to be a big help to your pa after you get a big wad o' greenbacks for investments."

"Damn right!" Tim agreed. He went back outside to the table and took an empty chair. "Finish the hand, boys," he said happily. "Then deal me in."

Curly Brandon, another of Big Ed's boys, studied his cards. "I'm warning you, Tim," he said good-naturedly. "I'm out to get even tonight. And my luck's running high and fast."

"Then my best wishes to you, Curly," Tim said.

Shorty clapped Tim on the shoulder. "We know you don't mean that!" He turned his attention back to the game. "I check to the pot."

"I raise a dollar," Hank Delong said. He too was a regular at the Deep River Saloon.

"Shit!" Shorty said, throwing in his cards.

"I'll see that dollar and raise another," Curly said.

"I can't quit now," Hank said, shoving in more money.

"Beat a full house," Curly said.

Hank grinned. "I reckon these four jacks'll do that just fine."

Now it was Curly who exclaimed, "Shit!"

The deal shifted to a man named Joe Black. He shuffled the cards and had them cut. "We'll try a little draw poker, boys. Ante up and open on what pleases you."

The cards were dealt, and for a minute each player studied the pasteboards. Shorty bet a dollar, and was matched all around.

"Cards?" Joe asked.

They took their cards. Tim had nothing special in his hand, but he asked for three. He ended up with a pair of sixes.

"You opened, Shorty," Joe said.

"Hell, you dealt me nothing," Shorty complained. "I'll check to the pot."

"You been doing that a lot," Curly said. "But I'll do the same."

"Sounds good to me," Hank said.

"And me," added Joe.

With nothing to lose, Tim went along.

"I got my eye on you," Hank said. "What've you got, boy?"

Tim grinned in embarrassment. "Only a pair o' sixes."

Everybody howled and threw in their cards. "Damn!" Hank said. "What lucky star was you borned under, boy?"

Tim raked in the money. "The North Texas Star, boys," he said with a laugh.

"Imagine winning on a lousy pair o' sixes," Shorty complained.

Hannah walked over with a bottle of rye and filled everyone's glasses. "Big Ed's in a good mood," she said. "He's buying, boys."

Tim said, "Go tell him I just won a pot on a pair o' sixes!"

"Sure, honey," Hannah said, walking away.

They played four more hands with Tim winning two of them. Hannah kept the rye flowing as the cards were dealt, played, dealt again, then studied once more to see who had the best hand for each pot.

Big Ed MacWilliams didn't pay much attention to the game. He went back to his chair on the porch and watched the town of Duncan ease into the new night. A few lantern lights came on, as did the ones inside the Deep River Saloon. Before long the entire street was dark except for the rays of illumination coming from windows.

A figure stepped from the gloom. "Howdy, Big Ed."

Big Ed turned to see a familiar face. "Howdy, Dan."

Sheriff Dan Sims glanced inside the barroom. "Seems kinda quiet."

"Just a poker game and somebody drinking real quiet," Big Ed said.

Sims nodded. He was a tall man in his forties. Rail-thin with thick black hair, he moved in a slow manner that suggested he was only relaxing before getting ready to explode into action. "Is young Tim Hawkins in there?"

"He sure is," Big Ed answered.

Sims grinned. "I reckon he's prob'ly doing real well at the game, ain't he?"

"I don't hear him complaining none," Big Ed answered.

"The boy has talent," Sims said. "Maybe he should

28

take up gambling as a profession."

"Maybe he should," Big Ed said. "Want to bankroll him?"

"That might not be a bad idea," the sheriff said. "I'll see you later. I got to make my early rounds."

"See you, Dan."

The game inside continued with occasional shouts and exclamations. Now and then either Rosalie or Hannah came out to keep Big Ed company. He always asked how the gambling was going.

"Tim Hawkins is cleaning 'em out again," Hannah said.

"Lucky boy," Big Ed said.

"Sure he is," Hannah said.

Big Ed studied the quiet, dark street that ran in front of his saloon. "Did you ever figure you'd come to this?"

"Come to what?" Hannah asked.

"Sitting in a little Texas town with nothing to do and no place to go," Big Ed answered.

Hannah shrugged. "What the hell! All I been worrying about all my life is getting that next bite o' food. Never mind where I been, where I am, or where the hell I'm going."

"Things is simple for you, Hannah," Big Ed said.

"Feeding myself is a simple thing to do," Hannah said. "And after all the hungry times I've had, it's the most important. Once I'm fed, I'm happy. Damn all the rest of it."

"Whoring feeds you so whoring is good, huh?"

"You damn right," Hannah said. She didn't like it when Big Ed started that kind of talk. "I'm going back in and watch the game."

She went back through the batwing doors and walked slowly up to the table. A thick cloud of smoke floated just above it as the intense poker players kept at their game. Rosalie Kinnon looked up at the older

29

woman, then turned her attention back to the contest.

More whiskey was poured as the time eased by. Finally Shorty Clemens stood up. "I'm busted," he announced. He abruptly left the table and went outside. He lit a cigar. "Things is winding down, Boss."

"Right," Big Ed said. He got out of his chair and took a slow stroll into the interior of the Deep River Saloon. He stood at the table and waited until the hand being played was finished.

"Gimme that money!" Tim Hawkins whooped, scooping his winnings toward him.

"Game's over," Big Ed announced.

"Aw! I'm going too good to quit," Tim protested.

"You can get more another night," Big Ed said. Without hesitating, he methodically picked up Tim's money. "I'll put it in the safe."

"Hell!" Tim said grinning drunkenly. "At least leave me a dollar to take Hannah upstairs."

Big Ed gave him the money, then headed back toward his office. "The last round is on me, boys."

While the players stumbled to the bar, the saloon owner continued on to the safe. Once more, as he had many times, he put all the money Tim had earned into his safe. By the time he went back outside, most of the lanterns were turned down as his men quietly sipped the liquor. Big Ed glanced upstairs toward the four rooms that opened on the landing.

A weak light came out from under Hannah's door.

Big Ed went to the bar, where he was served a drink from his own special bottle. Once more his thoughts turned to what a hell of a situation it was to be living there in the little town just off the Diablos Range.

Chapter 4

The scrambled eggs—hot, yellow, and steaming—were heaped onto the platter. Nancy Hawkins had gone out to the hen house and gathered them less than an hour earlier. After cooking the food, she'd piled it on a platter with bacon.

Rawley Pierson and Chaw Stevens waited in eager anticipation for the young girl to join them at the table after setting the skillet back on the stove. She retrieved a pan of hot biscuits and brought them to the table.

"Miss Nancy," Chaw said in pure delight. "I truly feel like I've died and went to heaven!"

"And we had such a delicious supper only last night too," Rawley added.

"Thank you," Nancy said. She liked to cook for appreciative, hungry folks. She sat down, and her father Zeb bowed his head. "Lord, we thank thee kindly for what we're about to receive. Amen."

"Amen," said Nancy.

The food was passed around. Tim's chair was noticeably empty. Zeb poured himself a deep cup of coffee, then gave the pot to Chaw. "Can't start the day without strong java."

"Them's the truest words spoke by man," Chaw said

in agreement. The whiskered old codger liked his coffee black, thick, and argumentative.

"This really is delicious, Miss Nancy," Rawley said. "It's been a long time since I've had biscuits this good."

"I'm glad you like them, Mr. Pierson," Nancy said smiling. "Sometimes we have trouble getting decent flour out here on the Diablos. Anyhow, it's a pleasure to cook for hungry men."

Rawley laughed. "Then you'll like cooking for Chaw. He's always hungry."

"That I am!" Chaw said, eating with gusto.

Although Nancy was delighted with the reaction to her cooking, she was bothered by her brother's absence. "Did you call Tim?" she asked her father.

"I did," Zeb answered angrily. "At least a half-dozen times. But I know he's up. I heard him stomping around in his boots."

Nancy said nothing, but the expression on her face plainly showed both anger and disappointment in her young brother. She stabbed at her eggs with her fork, eating rapidly.

"I reckon we'll be rounding up them cattle that was scattered yesterday," Rawley said, nibbling on a crisp piece of bacon.

"Yeah," Zeb Hawkins said. "That'll be finishing up the job that Jim and Duane started yesterday afore them bushwhackers moved in on 'em."

"We got to keep the herd closer to the ranch," Rawley said. "And mount a guard to keep watch."

"You're right about that," Zeb agreed. "But that would take stretching this little crew pretty far. That'd mean you, Chaw, Tim, and me would pull about six hours of guarding a day aside from doing the reg'lar range work. We'd be lucky to last out the week."

"I could help out, Papa," Nancy said.

"Honey, you got to fix grub for us and other things,"

Zeb pointed out. "And I don't think we'll be able to hire on a cook any more'n we can get more hands to work the herd."

"But I could at least put in two hours sometime in the middle of the night," Nancy insisted.

"I'll think on it," Zeb said.

Tim Hawkins stumbled into the room. His hair was slicked down but carelessly combed back, and it was evident he hadn't shaved. The young man said nothing as he sat down heavily in the chair opposite his father.

"How about a 'good morning, ever'body' from you?" Zeb said.

"Good morning, Pa—Nancy," Tim mumbled.

"Is Rawley and Chaw invisible?" Zeb asked.

Tim gave them a sullen look, then let his gaze sink to the tabletop.

"Want some eggs?" Nancy asked.

Tim shook his head. "Coffee. That's all."

"Get it yourself," she said.

Tim gave her a look of exasperation, but got to his feet and walked across the room to the stove. After returning to the table, he slurped a couple of swallows and moaned.

"You got a headache, boy?" Zeb asked.

"Yeah."

"Well, you better eat something," Zeb advised his son. "We got lots o' hard riding and rounding up to do today. We prob'ly won't have no noontime meal."

"I ain't hungry."

"I'll bet you ain't!" Zeb snapped, "That'll learn you to go into town drinking during the week."

Tim said nothing. He drank more coffee, wishing he could tell his father of the money in Big Ed MacWilliams's safe in the Deep River Saloon. In a couple of more months they'd have enough of a grubstake to get off the Diablos and into friendlier country to do their ranching.

Chaw, who was as fond of liquor as the next man, was amused by Tim's hangover. To the old range rider, a bad morning was a normal part of living. But he'd gone to sleep cold sober the previous night and his stomach growled for food. He noted the eggs left on the platter. "It'd be a shame to let them go to waste."

"Help yourself, Mr. Stevens," Nancy said.

"Thank you kindly, Miss," Chaw said. He dumped the entire amount on his plate and consumed it in three bites.

Tim groaned and rubbed his temples.

Zeb gave him a sharp look. "Are you gonna be able to ride today, boy?"

"Yes, sir," Tim said. "I always carry my weight, Pa."

Zeb nodded. "That you do. I can't fault you on that." He sighed. "Well, you're a man, so your own time is your own business. If you want to start out each day with a headache and an upset stomach, you go right ahead."

"He will," Nancy said.

Tim, feeling a bit better as the coffee pepped him up some, grinned at his sister. "Big Ed MacWilliams told me to say hello to you."

"I don't care what he said!" Nancy snapped.

Tim finished his coffee. "He's got a good business in town, sis. I'd say Big Ed does real good for hisself."

Nancy frowned furiously. She grabbed her empty plate and took it to the kitchen counter. Then she returned and angrily began clearing the table.

Now Tim was feeling better. "You ever notice how hard a woman starts working when she gets upset?"

Zeb stood up. "Well, speaking of work, boys. Let's go to it."

"I'm set," Rawley Pierson said.

The men got up and gave Nancy some final compliments on her cooking abilities, then headed directly for the corral to saddle up for the day's big chore.

"We'll find the herd up on the north side," Zeb said. "At least that's what I figger from what you told me about where the gunfight went on."

"Yes, sir," Rawley said. He threw his saddle over his horse's back and began cinching it down. "You reckon we'll meet them dry-gulchers again?"

"Hard to tell," Zeb answered. "They come and go as they please. We can get by for a coupla weeks without no trouble out on the Diablos Range. Then they come back with a vengeance. I just wish we could track down where they're hiding out."

"Do you think it's safe to leave Miss Nancy here by herself?" Rawley asked.

"So far they ain't hit no ranch houses," Zeb said. "All they want to do is keep the cattle scattered."

"Nancy can take care of herself," Tim said. "Don't worry about things that don't concern you, Pierson."

Zeb spoke up sharply. "Watch your tone! If it wasn't for Rawley and Chaw, that herd could have been run off a hell of a lot worse." He looked over at Rawley. "Nancy can shoot as good as any man. She can take care of herself."

"Glad to hear it," Rawley said. Under normal circumstances he might have carried the situation a bit farther with Tim. Rawley Pierson was not the type of man to take much guff off another. But out of respect for Zeb Hawkins he let the matter drop.

Chaw also kept quiet, but knew that the possibility of a blowup with the young hothead was in the offing.

After saddling up, the quartet galloped out of the ranch yard and headed out onto the Diablos to begin the search for the scattered Circle H Bar cattle.

After going a mile out onto the range, they spread out far in a line. Each man could barely see the other on

35

his flank as they rode easily across the rolling terrain that dipped and rose gently. It was a pleasant day with the warm spring sun gently basking the earth. A breeze, easy and intermittent, brought the scents of the reborn land with it. If it hadn't been for Nancy's strong coffee, the riders would have dozed off in their saddles as the morning drifted by.

But each man kept alert, his eyes searching the prairie for sign of the herd or some individual cattle that might have wandered a ways from their companions. Even then, the main body would be close by.

"Ho!"

The call from Tim Hawkins drifted and echoed across the prairie.

"Ho!" he shouted again. "There they are yonder!" He stood up in his stirrups and pointed to the northwest. After making sure he'd been seen and heard, the young man kicked his horse into a gallop.

Rawley, Chaw, and Zeb Hawkins followed. The ride took them into an arroyo and up the other side, where they broke out on another wide expanse of deep-grass country. The herd was there, held loosely together through bovine instinct as they grazed the lush countryside.

"Start out on the north and swing 'em south!" Zeb Hawkins yelled.

Rawley pulled on the reins and headed in that direction. Chaw, riding hard now, came in behind him, swinging out a bit. Off to the side, in toward the herd, Tim Hawkins leaned in his saddle as his own mount began the rounding-up process.

The cattle started to move then, the horsemen's actions heading them off in the right direction. Sensing they were about to be disturbed, some bawled and mooed as the movement began.

Tim reached the outermost point first and turned in

36

sharply, waving his hat. "Hyah! You sonofabitches! Hyah, you dogies!" he yelled.

On the opposite side, Zeb Hawkins held the herd in. In spite of his age, he rode hard and well as he stuck in the saddle as if born with it attached to his rump.

Now Rawley and Chaw were well situated in the drag position and they moved in. Chaw, happy to be a working cowboy again, joyfully yelped at the cattle, sounding like an excited collie dog.

"They're moving!" Zeb yelled. "Settle back!"

The herd was allowed to calm down some. Since the cattle headed in the right direction and could easily be controlled, the four-man crew eased their efforts in order to let the animals pick their own pace. Now and then a stray wandered out, but one of the riders quickly took care of the errant cow, forcing it back into the mass.

The ride out and roundup had taken longer than the crew realized. By the time they were halfway back to the ranch it was already mid-afternoon. The trail dust rose out of the grass, settling back on man and animal alike until it seemed as if they'd been sprinkled with a light cover of brown powder. Sweat from hat brims trickled down faces and stung their eyes. With the excitement over, the drovers treated their previously ignored thirst with deep drinks from canteens. Although the water had grown lukewarm since being drawn from the ranch well, it was as sweet as nectar to throats parched by hard, fast riding.

Zeb took the point to check out the direction they followed across the terrain. Tim and Chaw each rode flank while Rawley stayed in the drag position. Everything seemed routine and easygoing. Now the thoughts of hot supper a couple or so hours away began to drift into their minds. It had been eight hours since they'd devoured Nancy's eggs, bacon, and biscuits.

Rawley caught the movement up on the crest of a shallow hill to the north. A horseman showed himself as if by accident, quickly turning away to get out of sight. Rawley pulled his carbine from its boot. When two more men appeared he could easily see they wore hoods. He fired a quick shot.

"To the left!" he shouted.

A dozen riders now came into sight, firing rapidly as they charged down on the drovers and the cattle. The animals immediately bolted in panic, breaking into a run and turning toward the south.

Chaw, nearest the attackers, went for his pistol. Firing rapidly and defensively at them, the old man turned and headed in the same direction as the herd. Rawley and Zeb covered him as best they could as he galloped for safety. Out on the right flank, Tim Hawkins was forced to run with the cattle in order to avoid a collision that would throw him beneath the herd's heavy hooves.

The attackers spread out more, keeping up a steady staccato of fire. They concentrated their efforts on the unfortunate Chaw, who now gave up any chance of being able to effectively defend himself. He rode hell-for-leather in a slightly zigzagging course while Rawley and Zeb closed in on him. The pair fired at the pursuers to take some of the pressure off Chaw.

Within a short five minutes, the entire cattle drive had been blown completely to hell. The herd was scattered and running madly in a senseless, instinctive flight. Tim Hawkins was finally able to turn back to join his companions, but by the time he linked up with them the fight was over. The bushwhackers had turned and ridden off, the purpose of their attack accomplished.

Rawley shoved his carbine back in the boot. "Are you all right, Chaw?"

"Yeah," Chaw said. "They didn't hit me, but I'm damned if I know why not."

Zeb watched the last remnants of the herd disappear over the prairie. "All of today's work was for nothing."

"We ain't ever gonna get the herd to Kansas, Pa," Tim said. "Something's got to be done."

"It will be," Zeb said. "And there's only one way to do it."

"What do you have on your mind?" Rawley asked.

"Something that should've been did a coupla months ago. I'm gonna call together the rest o' the ranchers on the Diablos and form up to fight back," Zeb said.

Rawley knew how individualistic most ranchers were. "Do you think you can get 'em to agree to a single course of action and stick to it?"

Zeb shook his head and shrugged. "Who knows? I'll be the first to admit we're a hard-headed bunch. But we got to do something or this'll be the last season for any of us."

"It'll be dark afore we can round up the herd again," Tim said.

"Forget the herd," Zeb said. "Instead o' cattle, round up the ranchers on the Diablos. We'll have a meeting tomorrow on the Circle H Bar."

"What time you want 'em there?" Tim said.

"Make it high noon," Zeb said. "There ain't any sense in busting our butts out on the range till this thing is cleared up for good."

Tim galloped off to tend to the chore while Rawley, Chaw, and Zeb headed back for the ranch.

Chapter 5

The yard of the Circle H Bar was crowded with buckboards and horses by noon the next day.

Every rancher on the Diablos was there: Slim Watkins of the Lazy S; Doak Timmons, who ran the Diamond T; Fred Blevins, ramrod of the Double Box; and Ted Lawson, the Flying Heart owner.

Wives and kids also had arrived, making it a near-festive scene in spite of the seriousness of the meeting. Nancy Hawkins would have liked to stay with the men and discuss the problem of the raiders, but as first lady of the Circle H Bar, she was required to spend her time with the other women. The ladies quickly set up baskets of food with tables brought in the conveyances as a feast underwent quick organization.

The men, leaving the women to their chores, went inside the ranch house. Although the meeting was nowhere near a fancy occasion like a wedding or a funeral, and didn't call for any fancy duds, the rough men who moved into the living room were all dressed as if going to church.

Zeb Hawkins produced some liquor, and others added to the supply of intoxicants. Within a few minutes, the front of the house filled with cigar and

40

pipe smoke, while the ranchers consumed straight whiskey in large swallows.

Tim Hawkins sat off to one side while his father introduced Rawley Pierson and Chaw Stevens to the Diablos cattlemen. The cattlemen were a gruff, friendly group who gave firm handshakes and looked a man in the eye when they learned his name.

Zeb Hawkins gave everyone a chance to settle in a bit more before beginning the meeting. He went straight to the heart of the matter. "Gentlemen, we're on our last legs." He looked around from man to man. "Anybody want to argue about that?"

No one said anything. The type of men who settle into a wilderness to carve out cattle kingdoms for themselves did not like to admit anybody had pushed their backs to the wall.

"I ain't in an impossible situation," Ted Lawson said. "I just need a full crew to set things right."

"But you ain't got one," Zeb countered. "And you ain't gonna get enough hands neither." He pointed to Doak Timmons. "What about the Diamond T?"

"Same thing," Timmons said, smoking a cigar. "But at least my cook has stayed on." He chuckled. "That might not be much of a blessing for what's left o' my crew."

Zeb turned. "And the Lazy S and Double Box? Are you boys doing fine?"

"You know we ain't, Zeb," Fred Blevins said. "I've had two good cowboys kilt and the others left." He shook his head. "I can't hardly get enough help to run my damn chicken coop."

"Them raiders is eating us up one at a time," Zeb said. "And there ain't but one way to stop it. We got to quit being separate and get together and form us an association."

"I ain't much for belonging," Blevins said. "I always

41

liked doing things on my own."

"Goddamn it, Fred!" Zeb exclaimed. "So do I! I come out here to get away from crowds and towns and all them rules and agreements you got to have when you live and do business with a whole bunch o' people. But I'm getting run outta business by some masked sonofabitches I can't get my hands on. They come and go as they please, and now I can't even muster enough hands to herd cattle and fight back at the same time."

Rawley Pierson said, "The bushwhackers are trying to break up the roundups for the drive up to Kansas. They do just enough to keep the cattle scattered, then they pull back and wait for someone else to try to get organized."

"Hell, mister! We know that," Blevins said. "That's been going on out to the Double Box for the past six months."

"Don't it tell you something?" Rawley asked.

"Sure!" Blevins retorted. "Do you think I'm stupid? It tells me that someone's trying to ruin my damn ranch."

"It should tell you more'n that," Rawley said. "It should tell you that all these raiders are interested in is to break up the roundups to keep the cattle drives from starting. They ain't killing unless they have to, and they ain't hit the ranch houses yet, have they?"

"I reckon you're right," Watkins said. "The Lazy S is in one piece."

Blevins looked at Rawley. "If you're so smart, why do you think they want to keep us from making the drive up to Kansas this year?"

"I don't know that," Rawley said. "If I did, I could figger out who was doing it."

"What are you, a range detective or something?" Timmons of the Diamond T asked.

Chaw jumped in. "You just listen to him, mister!

42

When he was sheriff down to Benton, he figgered out a coupla robberies and a killing."

"I didn't come to the Diablos on purpose," Rawley said. "But now that I am here, I intend to stick around and help out."

"How come?" Watkins asked bluntly.

"That's my style," Rawley replied.

"And mine," Chaw added.

"Simmer down, ever'body," Zeb Hawkins said. "These two gents kept two of my cowboys from getting killed a coupla days ago. After they quit, Rawley and Chaw said they'd hire on to help out. And that's what they been doing. It ain't often you'll find a pair of fellers willing to jump in and help out strangers like this."

"I just wish I knowed for sure why all this is happening here on the Diablos," Doak Timmons said.

"It's a range war," Rawley said. "And you might as well face up to that fact. What you got here is an out-and-out range war."

"It ain't real wise to throw them two words around," Blevins said. "They got a terrible meaning."

"Right," Lawson agreed. "A range war is something that don't end quick or pleasant."

"You got one whether you like it or not," Rawley said.

"He's right, boys," Zeb said. "Just be glad we ain't fighting each other."

"If we was, we'd at least know who to shoot," Timmons suggested sarcastically.

"What the hell can we do about it?" Blevins asked. "We got a bunch o' masked strangers that outnumber us and are bound and determined to either run us off the Diablos or kill us doing it. And we can't find hide nor hair of 'em when we go out looking."

"Like I said before," Zeb remarked. "If we stay

separate from each other, they'll pick us off one by one. But if we get together, we're one big strong bunch it'd take an army to defeat."

Slim Watkins poured himself another drink. "You mean form a cattlemen's association?"

"I mean form the Diablos Range Cattlemen's Association," Zeb said.

"That is gonna take some discussion," Lawson said.

The group of rugged ranchers, though not sophisticated or particularly articulate, settled in with a natural practicality as they began to deliberate on the procedures necessary to organize a mutual-defense group.

Meanwhile, the ladies had already finished setting the tables for the outdoor meal. With calico cloths covering the food to keep the flies away, they settled down into little groups to exchange the latest gossip along with the exciting news of products available at both the general store and in the Sears Roebuck catalog that had arrived from the East.

Two riders rode into the ranch yard, considerably slowing down to avoid kicking up dust over the scene. They nodded to the ladies and politely tipped their hats. Big Ed MacWilliams and Sheriff Dan Sims took their horses up to the hitching post in front of the barn and dismounted.

Sims, his long face wearing its usual solemn expression, surveyed the sight in the ranch yard. "Almost looks like a hanging, don't it?"

"All we need is a gallows," Big Ed said. "Sure you ain't got a pris'ner we could haul out here and string up?"

Sims, who didn't like jokes, made no reply.

Big Ed looked around, and spotted Nancy Hawkins speaking with some other ladies at one of the tables near the barn. "Wait here," he told Sims. The bar owner walked through the small crowd, and removed his hat as he walked up to the young woman. "Howdy, Miss Nancy."

Nancy turned. Her smile faded at the sight of the big man. "How do you do, Mister MacWilliams?"

"I'm fine, thank you kindly," he said. "Hello, ladies."

The two women, Nora Watkins and Penny Blevins, merely nodded. Being frontier women, they felt no snobbishness toward MacWilliams because of any social standing, but they didn't approve of saloons that separated poor, drunken cowboys from their miserable wages. They quickly excused themselves, leaving Nancy and Big Ed alone.

"Looks like quite an occasion," Big Ed said.

"The ranchers have finally decided to fight back against the masked cowards that have been attacking us," Nancy said. Then she quickly added, "What brings you out here, Mister MacWilliams?" She noted Dan Sims standing over by the horses. "And with the sheriff."

"We heard about the meeting," Big Ed explained. "As it happens, I may have a solution to offer. And, of course, Sheriff Sims is inter'sted in law and order out on the Diablos."

"But not interested enough to come out and give us a hand fighting the raiders," Nancy quickly added.

"He's only one man with a part-time deputy, Miss Nancy," Big Ed said. "There ain't a lot he can do."

"He could do more," Nancy said.

"Maybe," Big Ed allowed. He gestured at the picnic-like scene. "Sure seems like a pleasant enough afternoon, don't it?"

"If you have an answer to the problem, perhaps you should go in and discuss it with the men," Nancy said coldly.

Big Ed nodded. "I reckon you're right. It was nice

45

talking to you."

"Good day, Mister MacWilliams."

Big Ed walked toward the house, signaling Sheriff Sims to join him. Sims looked over at Nancy, who had rejoined the women. "I don't think that gal cottons to you, Big Ed."

"Maybe not now," Big Ed said confidently. "But she will by and by."

"Are you sure of that?"

"Where things concern me, I'm always sure," Big Ed said. "C'mon. Let's see what them ranchers is up to."

The pair walked up to the porch of the ranch house, and tapped on the front door before walking in. All the ranchers gave Big Ed a friendly greeting. His Deep River Saloon was their only recreation for drinking, card-playing, and some dallying now and then with one of the girls working there. Sheriff Dan Sims got a colder, yet polite reception.

"I hear you boys have decided to finally do something about the range raiders," Big Ed said.

"We sure have," Zeb answered. "We just now formed up the Diablos Range Cattlemen's Association." He held up two pieces of paper covered with writing. "And we writ down some of the rules and agreement we're gonna foller."

"Well, gents," Big Ed said with a wide grin. "I could have saved you all that trouble if'n I'd got here sooner. I got a damn good answer to your problem."

The group was interested. Sheriff Sims stayed by the door while Big Ed strode up to the front of the room where Zeb Hawkins stood.

"What the hell's on your mind, Big Ed?" Slim Watkins asked.

"I got a letter from an old pard o' mine," Big Ed said. "I ain't seen him since we run a place down in San Angelo a few years ago. When we sold the place, he

46

took his money and went back East where he come from." Big Ed laughed. "I reckon the cowboys unsettled him some."

"They can do that!" Fred Blevins said with a guffaw.

"At any rate, he got hisself into a real estate firm and he's been doing real good in New York," Big Ed went on. "Him and his comp'ny has decided to expand and they're looking for some land investments out West." He paused and peered around as if looking for eavesdroppers. "Gents," Big Ed continued in a subdued voice, "I know for a fact you can get a good price for your spreads out on the Diablos. You could take them profits and go somewhere that bushwhackers ain't running wild and taking over. Hell! Let them smart Eastern dudes have to deal with 'em."

Zeb Hawkins held up his hand. "Hold on, Big Ed! You don't seem to understand something. In the first place, them bushwhackers ain't taking over."

"Well, now, Zeb," Big Ed said. "I didn't mean—"

"And none of us come out here and busted our asses in the boiling summer and freezing winter to sell out and go somewheres else," Zeb said.

"That's right," Fred Blevins said, echoing the sentiment. "These here are our ranches and we damn well mean to keep 'em and work 'em till eternity splits open the Texas sky!"

"Gents, you're missing out on a good chance," Big Ed said. "Them Eastern fellers is rich and have got more money than good sense."

"And we got more guts than good sense," Zeb said. "And from this moment on, the Diablos Range Cattlemen's Association is gonna use pistols and carbines to put a final end to them bushwhackers and their game."

"Enough said!" Doak Timmons yelled. "We're formed up and ready to go. The ladies has got food waiting,

47

and there's more liquor too. This is cause for a celebration." He looked around. "Ted, did you bring your fiddle?"

"I sure did," Ted Lawson of the Flying Heart Ranch answered. "And my boy has got his accordion."

Yelping now in the Texas tradition, the crowd abruptly went outside to begin the festivities. Zeb took Big Ed's arm. "You're welcome to join us." He looked at the sheriff. "You too, Dan."

"I got things to tend to," Big Ed said. "Thanks just the same."

Rawley Pierson and Chaw Stevens were the last to leave the house. They walked behind Zeb Watkins as he stepped off the porch. The three watched Big Ed and Dan Sims mount up and ride away. As they rode out the gate, two more horsemen came in.

"Damn my eyes!" Zeb Hawkins said. "Look who's back!"

Jim Pauley and Duane Wheeler, the two cowboys, came up. They reined in and looked down from their saddles with sheepish grins.

"Howdy, Mister Hawkins," Duane said. "Me and Jim was wondering if we could have our jobs back."

"We felt real bad about walking out on you like that," Jim added. "We'd be proud if you'd call us Circle H Bar hands again."

"Hell, yes!" Zeb said. "And you're as welcome as can be."

Duane and Jim nodded to Rawley and Chaw. Duane said, "What made us change our minds 'bout leaving was thinking of you two staying on. That kinda shamed us. You don't mind us riding with you, do you?"

"We'd be proud," Rawley said.

"You bet!" Chaw added. He nudged Rawley. "By God! There ain't nothing like a coupla proud, honest cowboys. You'd never see nobody like that in a town."

"You're right," Rawley said.

"By damn!" Zeb said happily. "Getting them two back and having the cattlemen's association means things is really starting on the Diablos now."

"That's right," Rawley said. "A range war."

Zeb looked at him. "If that's what it takes."

Rawley nodded. "That's what it takes."

Chapter 6

The big, complicated task of organizing the Diablos Range Cattlemen's Association slowed down normal ranching activities. A lot of last-minute agreements and arguments had to be ironed out by the new organization's five highly individualistic and expressive ranchers. Plenty of quarreling and cuss words marked the occasion before the stubborn cattlemen reached that final settlement they were all willing to sign and—most importantly to them—shake hands on.

While the owners stormed and raged, their crews of drovers took advantage in the lapse of activity to enjoy some well-earned relaxation. With work down to a low level and a couple of easy days in the offing, Rawley Pierson and Chaw Stevens decided to go into town and check out what pleasures and diversions in the Deep River Saloon had to offer to a couple of weary drovers. After those two weeks on the trail and a few days of hard ranch work, the pair of friends needed to ease up and take a breather.

But they stuck around the ranch at least long enough for one of Nancy's suppers. Good grub was something not to be passed up even when there was a real strong hankering to blow off some steam. After wolfing down the food and mumbling quick compliments to the young woman, they wasted no time in saddling up and riding off the Diablos.

Rawley had gone to the trouble of taking a bath before eating, which was something Chaw would never do. As they continued toward town, Chaw looked over at him and remarked, "You're as about as slicked down as a drowning coyote, ain't you?"

"A man has to groom now and then," Rawley said, noting Chaw's unkempt beard.

"Only if he don't stay out on a good ol' cattle range," Chaw pointed out. "Them dogies don't give a damn about how you smell or look, and that's a fact."

Rawley grinned over at his pard as their horses loped toward the hamlet. "I don't care what you say. I see that you got no dislike of town now."

"Damn it, Rawley!" Chaw sputtered. "I never said I didn't ever want to go into no towns. I just growed tired of living in 'em."

Rawley grinned and settled into the saddle. It was a five-mile ride from the Circle H Bar before they crossed the limits of Duncan, Texas. He took advantage of the time to keep Chaw riled up with plenty of remarks about the older man's attitudes toward civilization and other people in general.

When they reached their destination, the pair found that the town was a small place with a combination of rickety adobe and frame buildings. A blacksmith, livery stable, jail, the Deep River Saloon, and a general store, whose owner also acted as the town barber, made up the small commercial district that formed a short main street. The residences were in a sort of disorderly arrangement behind that part of the prairie burg.

"Ain't much of a town," Rawley remarked. He'd

hoped it might have been at least close in size to the place where they'd been sheriff and deputy.

"It's got a saloon, ain't it?" Chaw asked.

"Yep."

"Then it's a mighty fine town," Chaw insisted. "At least it's all the town I need."

Rawley laughed as they came to a stop in front of Big Ed MacWilliams's place. They stepped out of their saddles and tied the horses to the hitching rail.

Big Ed, in his usual place on the porch, looked at them from his chair. "Howdy. You're the fellers off'n the Circle H Bar, ain't you?"

"That's right," Chaw said coldly. He hadn't liked Big Ed when he'd first seen him in the Hawkinses' living room the day the association was formed. As far as Chaw was concerned, the large man represented the worst type of town people.

"I remember you," Big Ed said. "You're the helpful ones, ain't you?"

"We try to be," Rawley said. He wasn't quite sure what Big Ed meant by the question, but it didn't seem delivered in a particularly friendly manner.

"I ain't good with names. I'm Ed MacWilliams. Folks around here call me Big Ed."

"I'm Rawley Pierson and this here's my pard Chaw Stevens," Rawley said.

"Where's Tim?" the saloon owner asked.

"He's with his pa at a meeting over to the Double Box spread," Rawley answered.

"Sounds like them ranchers is plowing ahead with their plans for an association," Big Ed said.

"You can count on that," Rawley said. "Matter o' fact, they're about ready to shake and sign on it."

"That must mean they're real serious," Big Ed said.

Chaw pointed to the interior of the establishment.

"You got whiskey in there, mister?"

"I do," Big Ed answered.

"Then we'll go drink some," Chaw announced. "C'mon, Rawley."

Rawley followed the little man inside. They went straight to the bar, and Chaw banged on it. Roy Patton, the bartender, came over and waited to hear their pleasure.

"Whiskey," Chaw said. "The bottle and two glasses."

"Coming up pronto, gents," Patton said. He fetched what was ordered and came back, setting it all down in front of the whiskered oldster. "That's four bits in coin or a dollar in paper."

"How much will a Confederate dollar get me?" Chaw asked, eyeing the barkeep carefully.

Patton said nothing. He simply looked into Chaw's face without changing his expression.

Chaw was persistent. "There was a time and a place when that money was good enough."

"The time and place ain't here or now," Patton said.

Chaw nudged Rawley. "Give him a Yankee dollar."

Rawley paid up and grabbed the bottle, pouring them each a glassful. He raised his own. "Here's to fast horses and perty women."

"Just a minute!" Chaw protested. "You're always drinking to the same thing." He thought a moment. "Here's to perty horses and fast women." He cackled and drank.

Rawley appreciated the taste of the liquor even if it was cheap and unaged. "It's been a while since we eased back."

"That is has," Chaw allowed. "I reckon the night after we turned in our badges and rode outta Benton was the last time. That's been over two weeks."

"If we get on any trail drives, we'll go a hell of a lot

53

more'n two weeks without any relaxation," Rawley said. "A feller can go a month or so then without having any fun in town."

"But he's out in the open country, Rawley!" Chaw exclaimed. "And a man don't need whiskey when he's working hard and free with nobody breathing down his neck but a damn trail boss. All he's got to do to keep the peace is put in a good day's work."

"That's right enough. But there's also Injuns and rustlers too at times," Rawley pointed out.

Chaw chuckled. "Well, pard, that's the spice in that bowl o' soup, ain't it?"

"Pour us another drink," Rawley said.

They quickly downed that one and served themselves a third. Rawley felt a tug on his arm, and turned to see that a saloon girl had joined them. He tipped his hat. "Howdy."

"Howdy," Rosalie Kinnon said. "Will you buy a girl a drink?"

Chaw looked across his friend at her. "We'll give you one out of our own bottle," he said testily. "I don't like paying for a glass half filled with water when I slide money across a damn bar."

"We aim to keep the customers happy here at the Deep River," Rosalie said with a smile. She snapped her fingers at Patton. "Bring me a glass, Roy."

Patton obliged. Rosalie pushed the glass toward Chaw. "Fill 'er up!"

Chaw did as she asked. "Just 'cause I made a gentlemanly offer don't mean you got a claim on this bottle."

Rosalie knocked the drink back in a quick swallow. "I don't need watered-down stuff, mister. I can drink likker as good as any man."

"I'll give you another if you'll drink it slow," Rawley said.

"Sure, mister," Rosalie replied. She liked the handsome stranger. He had a nice smile and an easy manner. And he didn't smell bad either. She was always more comfortable with cowboys who'd taken the trouble to bathe before hitting town. "My name's Rosalie."

"Howdy, Rosalie," Rawley said. "I'm called Rawley and this is my pard Chaw."

"Howdy, miss," Chaw said sullenly.

Rosalie ignored the older man. She moved closer to Rawley. "You looking for a good time?"

"Sure," Rawley said. "After I've had a few drinks."

"Then I'll come back and see you later," she said, winking. "I don't want to hog your whiskey."

"You won't!" Chaw said. "I'll see to that personal, missy."

Rosalie brushed up against Rawley with her hips before she walked away.

"I'm glad I've aged past all that," Chaw said. "When I think o' the trouble and money and time I've wasted on women, it pure makes me sick."

Rawley thought of Nancy. She'd been in his mind quite a bit, but sometimes a man's needs were handled better in an upstairs room with a saloon gal. "You shoulda got married, you ol' goat."

"I could have," Chaw said. "I was a real good-looking feller when I was young."

"You were, huh?"

"Yeah," Chaw said. "As a matter o' fact, I was better-looking then than you are now."

"Yeah?"

"Yeah. The gals was always after me," Chaw said smugly. "Back when I was a Johnny Reb—and I still am one—more 'n one lady said I was the best-looking soljer in General John B. Hood's division."

"Ain't that the outfit that scared most damn Yanks

to death 'cause they was so ugly?" Rawley asked, suppressing a grin.

"Who tole you that?" Chaw demanded. "Why we was the best-looking fellers that wore rebel gray. Why we was—"

"All right, Chaw," Rawley said. "I was just funning you."

"Imagine that!" Chaw said after he took another drink. "Accusing General John B. Hood's boys o' being ugly! A couple might've been close, but I reckon the worse of 'em was at least tolerable."

Rawley poured himself some more whiskey, then turned and looked outward at the barroom. He quietly surveyed the tables, noting the various drinkers and cardplayers. He nudged Chaw. "There's some hard-cases in here."

Chaw took a quick look. "Yeah. You're right. Guns is wore low and they look like they might use 'em for a living, huh?"

"I reckon it takes a coupla ex-star-packers to figger that out," Rawley said. The years he'd spent as a lawman had given him a pretty good ability to sort out troublemakers when he walked into a dangerous situation, or even a quiet saloon like the Deep River.

"I wonder what they're doing around here," Chaw said. "You wouldn't think Big Ed pulled in enough money to keep a pistolero payroll, would you? And even if he did, why'd the big sumbitch want or need one?"

"You don't suppose they got anything to do with them hooded fellers, do you?" Rawley asked.

Chaw shook his head. "These boys ain't spent much time outdoors. From the looks of 'em, I'd say they stick around here perty close. And I noticed a coupla of 'em hobnobbing with that feller Big Ed."

"Maybe they're his boys after all," Rawley said.

"What the hell for?" Chaw asked.

Rawley shrugged and turned around to give the bottle some more of his attention. The liquor was warm in his belly and he felt a glow from it. A man, whether working for the law or a rancher, needed time to knock back a few drinks now and then to get the kinks out of his mind and let his body relax a bit.

Rosalie Kinnon sided up to Rawley. "Ready for that good time yet?"

Rawley grinned, feeling a little drunk. "I'm getting there."

Rosalie looked over at Chaw. "What about you? Hannah ain't busy."

"Well, I am!" Chaw said. "With this here bottle."

Rawley started to laugh, but a masculine voice interrupted him. "C'mon with me, Rosalie."

Rosalie turned and looked at Curly Brandon. "I'm with this gent right now, Curly."

He grabbed her arm and pulled the girl roughly to him. "No you ain't."

"What's the matter with you?" Rosalie demanded. "Leave me be!"

Rawley, feeling agitated by the man's brashness, stepped back from the bar. "I was fixing to buy the little lady a drink."

"Ain't nobody asking you nothing," Curly sneered. "So don't say nothing."

Rawley's stubborn nature came to the surface. "The lady obviously wants to be with me, and I like her comp'ny. So move on."

Curly shoved Rosalie away. "Nobody tells me to move on."

"Now is that gospel truth?" Rawley said with a lazy grin. "I swear that I just did. In case you didn't hear it the first time, I'll say it again. *Move on.*"

Curly moved with an explosive speed as he stepped forward and threw a punch. But Rawley, set and ready, went under it and came up with an uppercut that caught Curly full on the jaw.

Curly's eyes went blank and he stumbled back, falling to the floor. Hank Delong made a sudden appearance from the side, charging straight into Rawley. But Chaw intercepted him with a vicious kick that caught the side of his knee. Howling, Hank hopped away, and Rawley finished him off with a vicious sideswipe that spun him around and dumped him to fall beside Curly.

The room was suddenly quiet. Rawley and Chaw, with pistols drawn, stood ready for action. Their quick but careful glances around the room showed no more troublemakers moving their way.

Big Ed MacWilliams stood by the door flanked by Shorty Clemens and Joe Black. He smiled and walked over to Rawley. He motioned for Shorty and Black to take care of the fallen men.

Big Ed took a pull off his cigar. "I'm right embarrassed that something like that happened in my place."

"I hope you don't lose no sleep over it," Rawley said. He and Chaw reholstered their irons.

"I just might," Big Ed said. He looked over at the bartender. "Roy, give these boys a drink on the house. That's the least I can do."

"Yes, sir."

Rosalie walked up. "That damn Curly started pushing me around, Big Ed. And for no damn good reason."

"I'll take care of Curly," Big Ed said. "You go ahead and entertain Rawley Pierson here."

Rosalie smiled. Once more she moved close to

58

Rawley. "You said you wanted my comp'ny. Here or upstairs?"

"Upstairs," Rawley said. "Fighting gets my blood up."

Chaw watched the couple head up for the rooms on the second floor. He poured himself a drink, and wisely turned around to keep an eye out on the scene before him. He drank slowly, noting that the two men who had been manhandled by Rawley and him were sitting at a table. Chaw loosened the Colt in his holster, his growing tenseness overcoming the effect of the whiskey. He still hadn't relaxed any when Rawley and Rosalie came back down.

"Let's go on back to the ranch," Chaw said.

Rawley nodded. "We might as well since you drank the last o' the likker." He patted Rosalie on the rump. "I'll be back, hear?"

"You bet!"

The two men walked easily but tensely toward the door. Once outside, they quickly got into the saddle. Instead of riding directly out of town, they circled around to the back of the business district, then set out onto the Diablos on a route nobody would expect them to take. There was no sense in giving any potential bushwhacker an advantage.

"I'll tell you something," Chaw said seriously. "There's more going on in that Deep River Saloon than can be seen on the surface."

"I think so too," Rawley said. "Them two jaspers was set on us. They was real businesslike about it."

"Hell, that was easy to see," Chaw said. "They didn't even act mad after it was all said and done. Normal brawlers would've gone to gunplay. Them boys is professionals. I'll wager they even got a extry dollar or two for jumping us. And another thing I'll bet on is that

59

it's Big Ed that calls their play."

"Yeah," Rawley agreed. "I can tell you one thing for sure, though. There's a hell of a lot of strange things gonna happen before we ride off this Diablos Range."

"Yeah," Chaw said thoughtfully. "Strange and dangerous."

Chapter 7

The five outfits running cattle on the Diablos wasted no time in following the agreements of their association. The ranches—the Circle H Bar, Lazy S, Diamond T, Double Box, and Flying Heart—all entered into the spirit of their consolidation with grim determination.

The main thrust of the organization was to bring all herds together into one large group for the drive to Kansas. This would make guarding the cattle easier, although a chance of mixing the animals was a possibility. The ranchers decided it was worth the risk of somebody losing a few head.

"It'll all work out in the end anyhow," Zeb Hawkins pointed out to his friends. "And let's face it, boys. A few head is gonna get mixed up with some others. It's gonna be more'n a month afore we're ready to head north."

They all agreed with Zeb, realizing that worrying over who owned certain cattle had to be put in the background while they concentrated on the important job of the inevitable roundup and branding that had to be done.

By concentrating all their resources in a communal

effort, not only would the brutal work ahead go more quickly and efficiently, but in case of attack, there would be a better chance of finally tracking down the raiders to their lair. But Fred Blevins of the Double Fox remained pessimistic.

"They'll start fighting us in differ'nt ways, boys, and prob'ly get their edge back in this game," he said. Then he quickly added, "But maybe we'll be on our way to Kansas by that time."

"Maybe and maybe not," Fred Blevins said. "The situation is just like Zeb said. It's gonna take over a month o' quiet grazing to fatten them critters up enough for the drive north."

"You're forgetting something else that's in our favor," the Diamond T's Doak Timmons quickly pointed out. "By getting together, we can work with short-handed crews a hell of a lot better."

Zeb Hawkins summed it up but without modesty. "My idea o' forming this cattleman's association was a damn good one! Now that we all agree on that, let's stop jawing and get this here roundup started."

Following a planning session on the Double Box, a composite work crew, a total of fifteen men in all, rode out on the Diablos and began gathering the drifting herds, moving them toward a central spot just north of Doak Timmons's Diamond T at a place called Rattlesnake Arroyo.

When they came across strays, the crew picked them up as well, adding them to the growing crowd of cattle as they concentrated on the difficult task that faced them.

After a day and half of riding, herding, reherding, and chasing, a sizable crowd of bawling cattle had been assembled around the huge gully. A fire of hot coals had been built up, and the branding irons of the Circle H Bar, Lazy S, Diamond T, Double Box, and Flying

Heart grew glowing red in the awesome heat.

It was old Zeb Hawkins who, as he usually did, got things moving after everyone had instinctively settled down when the rounding-up was finished.

"What the hell are you waiting for? Ropers! Get your lazy butts to work!" Zeb bellowed. "Them calves ain't gonna sashay over on their own to get branded!"

Rawley Pierson and Tim Hawkins formed one of the roping teams. Riding into the herd with their lariats ready, they looked for unbranded calves. Rawley spotted the first one. Honing skills that had lain dormant for nearly three years, he cut the young animal loose from his mother, driving him out of the bovine crowd. A quick toss of the rope and the calf was dragged to the fire. Jim Pauley and Duane Wheeler off the Circle H Bar grabbed the animal and wrestled him to the ground.

Chaw Stevens had been detailed as the brander. "Which outfit?" he asked.

"Diamond T," Rawley answered.

Chaw grabbed the correct brand and hurried over to the struggling calf, applying the instrument with a vicious shove. Burning hair and flesh stunk up the immediate vicinity.

"It's a male," Duane Wheeler said.

Jim Pauley chuckled. "He won't be for long."

Chaw pulled his knife from his scabbard and quickly cut off the unfortunate animal's testicles. After an application of creosote, the calf was allowed to scramble back into the herd and look for his mother, bewildered and bawling in a great deal of pain.

Rawley rode back into the herd, looking for another. A couple of more ropers dragged their struggling victims over for Chaw's less-than-tender treatment. It was the start of a sweating, straining routine as the air was filled with oaths, shouts, bleats of calves, and bad smells.

The work was hard and the men strained their muscles to the limit as the roping, wrestling, and branding continued throughout the morning under a sun that grew hotter with each passing hour.

The high point of the whole affair was the chuck wagon. Nancy Hawkins had agreed to fill in for the Diamond T's cook, who'd been dispatched to pick up grub in town. She was as adept at cooking over an open fire as she was an iron stove. The young woman baked bread and concocted a stew of beef, vegetables, chili peppers, and potatoes that produced an odor so pleasing that stomachs began growling for the food hours before mealtime.

Finally, when the sun was at its zenith, Nancy banged on the gong hanging from the chuck wagon's roof. The lucky cowboys able to eat first wasted no time in rushing for the food. Others, less fortunate, who had been detailed to act as lookouts, had to wait on the edge of the roundup area and keep their eyes peeled for any hooded raiders that might make an appearance.

Rawley and Chaw were among the first to be fed. Grabbing tin plates and spoons, they lined up with the others and walked past the wagon as Nancy served the thick stew with a biscuit on top.

"How're you doing, Miss Nancy?" Rawley inquired as he got his grub.

"I'm fine, thank you, Mister Pierson," she answered with a bright smile. "I've been watching you work. You're a good roper."

Chaw, standing behind Rawley, chimed in. "He was practical borned with a rope in his hands, miss. He's a Texas cowboy tried and true!"

Nancy nodded. "I believe that."

The pair of friends walked off a ways and sat down

on the ground to consume the feast. Chaw took a mouthful and chewed thoughtfully before he spoke. "She's sweet on you."

"Who?"

"Who?" Chaw sputtered. "The Queen of the May!" He shook his head. "I'm a-talking about Miss Nancy, o'course."

"She ain't sweet on me," Rawley said.

"Oh, yeah? Look at the differ'nce in the amount of food you got and what the others—and me—is getting."

"She admired ropers," Rawley said, grinning. But he had noted that she'd given him a whopping helping of the stew.

Chaw eyed him suspiciously. "You ain't finding her on the perty side, are you?"

"Sure," Rawley said. "Any damn fool can see she's a perty woman. You think I'm blind?"

"No," Chaw said. "But I think you could be got into a woman's trap real careful."

"Pshaw!"

"You ain't real bright when it comes to women," Chaw insisted. He was thoughtful. "O'course you ain't real bright about a lotta things. But women is gonna be your downfall, mark my words."

"I suppose you're a real expert on women, huh?" Rawley said. "You ain't ever been married before, so how come you know so much about 'em?"

"That," Chaw said leaning forward, "is because I'm just like you said—a expert on females and have avoided their tricks. How do you think I managed to keep my freedom all these long years?"

Zeb Hawkins's voice thundered over the scene, interrupting them. "Goddamn it! Let's eat up, boys! There's lots o' work and the lookouts is got to be fed!"

Although the food was gone and deserved to be

savored, Zeb and the other four ranch owners had no patience with any gourmets in the crowd. Continuing to cuss and complain, Hawkins and his colleagues made the men eat as fast as possible. The first who finished their platefuls were immediately sent out to relieve the sentries. Within thirty-five minutes of the gong's first sounding, the work resumed with as much noise and ruckus as before.

The day's heat increased even more in the afternoon, leaving the drovers soaked in sweat with physical fatigue rapidly growing. The roping became sloppier, and it took more time for the riders to cut the unbranded calves loose from the herd. But everyone pressed on, knowing that time was their biggest enemy. The herd had to be carefully guarded while fattening up on the lush prairie grass. Then there was that long drive up into Kansas still awaiting them after all this backbreaking, butt-busting labor.

The first shot blasted over the noise of the bustling activities when the afternoon's shadows were lengthening steadily toward evening.

"Raiders!" came a cry from the edge of the workplace.

Everyone knew what to do. Five of the men turned their full attention to the cattle to avoid a stampede if possible. Rawley Pierson led the others on an impromptu all-out attack against the marauders.

The hooded bushwhackers, numbering at least two dozen, were in a tight formation as they pounded in toward the herd. Their firing, while aimed at the cowboys, was as much for disturbing the herd as it was for killing anybody.

But the five cowboys, following the preconceived plan, drove the cattle toward Rattlesnake Arroyo, to use its confining walls of earth to keep the excited animals under control.

Rawley and the others cut in between the big gully and the attackers, adding to the distance between them and the herd. Now shooting regularly toward the masked men, ten guns blasted slugs among the raiders, the reports blending in with the thundering of hooves on the prairie ground.

One spoiler rolled over his horse's rump and bounced heavily to the dirt as the cattlemen's bullets swarmed into the crowd. His pals, surprised by the organized defense, were game to keep the fight going, however. They turned inward, closing in with the men they outnumbered.

Both groups, firing wildly, galloped head on toward each other. Now caught up in the excitement, all the battle's participants whooped and hollered as their rage built. The air was split with flying bullets, and the horses sensed the combination of anger and fear from their riders and their own spirits turned vicious.

The cowboys enjoyed a distinct advantage in the opening volleys that continued as both groups grew closer. The intruders, more numerous and riding close together, made a composite target that could be easily fired into without careful aiming. The drovers, on the other hand, were scattered and loose, with large areas of empty space between each horseman.

Three of the invaders simultaneously pitched from their saddle, then two more went down. The sight of five of their number suddenly shot from their horses unnerved the rest of the gang. Although there was no communication between them, each cut loose with a final fusillade before turning away and making a beeline for the safety of the open range.

But those final shots cut down two cattlemen.

Rawley, with instincts and attitudes built up during his service as a lawman, wanted to chase after the invaders. But his horse, like the others, had been worked hard all that day, and couldn't keep up with the fresher ones the invaders rode. Reluctantly he turned back.

Rawley noted the men dismounted and gathered in a small group. He rode over to see what was the matter. He rightly figured they were gathered around the casualties, and he was relieved to see that Chaw Stevens was unhurt among the drovers as he reined up.

A cowboy off the Flying Heart was getting his lightly wounded arm wrapped up by his bunkies. Rawley urged his mount past the crude doctoring to join the group which included all the Circle H Bar men. He dismounted and pushed his way in.

Tim Hawkins knelt beside his father. Old Zeb, his chest a bloody mess, stared sightlessly up into the Texas sky. That long, long trip he'd taken out from Kentucky with a new bride and high hopes had finally come to an end.

The other ranch owners joined the crowd. Each man respectfully removed his hat and looked down on the corpse of a rancher they admired and respected.

It was Doak Timmons off the Diamond T who spoke aloud what everybody was thinking. "Now we got an even better reason than pertecting our ranches to kill them sonofabitches."

Tim tried to exhibit self-control, but was having a hard time. He started to say something, but choked up.

Rawley knew what to do. He went to Zeb's horse and untied the bedroll from the back of the saddle. He unrolled the blankets, spreading them out. Several of the men gently picked up Zeb and laid him down on the covers. They were closed over him and tied at both ends. Then the old man's body was lifted up and laid across the saddle, the ends of the blankets lashed to the stirrup straps to keep the corpse from slipping off.

Rawley gently took Tim's arm and eased him up to

68

his feet. "We'll take your pa back to the ranch. Go over to the chuck wagon and tell Miss Nancy. You can't take her home."

Tim took a deep breath, then nodded. "I know what I gotta do, Pierson. I ain't a wailing kid."

Rawley's jaw tightened, but under the circumstances he made no reply to the arrogant remark.

After Tim rode off toward Rattlesnake Arroyo, Jim Pauley and Duane Wheeler mounted up to begin the slow trek back to the Circle H Bar with the dead man.

Rawley and Chaw went with the others to the outlaws' bodies that lay scattered across the range. Each was dead, and the hoods they wore were ripped roughly from off their heads. The features, cold and dead, were unrecognizable to any of the ranchers and cowboys. But Rawley and Chaw recognized one of them.

"That's Jack Freeman!" Chaw exclaimed when the mask was removed.

"Sure is," Rawley agreed. "We ain't seen him in more'n two years."

Ted Lawson, owner of the Flying Heart, was curious. "Where'd you fellers know him from?"

"We had a run-in with him while we was star-packers down in Benton," Rawley explained. "He's a bad'un that hires out his gun when he ain't getting into mischief on his own."

"I reckon if he's a professional pistolero so are these others," surmised Fred Blevins of the Double Box.

"Somebody's got enough money to pay for more'n two dozen hardcases," Rawley said. "And that's not for a single job, that's to keep 'em around for a long period of time."

"You suppose this is a gang?" Slim Watkins asked.

Rawley shook his head. "There ain't no bandit chief that can keep his men inter'sted in a long job that don't produce cash money."

"Yeah," Chaw agreed. "Especially when they can't go to town and let off steam now and then."

Chaw Stevens looked over at the ranchers. "You gents has got some powerful enemies."

"What we got is a range war," Slim Watkins of the Lazy S said.

"And it's gonna get worser," sadly commented the Diamond T's Doak Timmons.

Chapter 8

Zeb Hawkins had to be buried quick. Between the bloody, flesh-tearing mortal wound he'd received in his chest and the rapidly warming weather, there was no way his corpse could be kept long without a proper undertaker's care. And no such services were available in the nearby town of Duncan. The only thing that could be done for the dead man was to slip his Sunday-go-to-meeting suit on to cover the massive injury and make him as presentable as possible for the funeral.

Young Tim Hawkins, wanting to spare his sister as much as possible, took on that job himself. After dressing his father for the burial, he took the blood-soaked clothes the old man had died in and burned them behind the bunkhouse.

The cowhand Jim Pauley was a fair carpenter, and he wasted no time in putting together a coffin from lumber in the Circle H Bar ranch barn. It was padded with a quilt from Zeb's bed. His first wife, the young girl from his native state of Kentucky, had laboriously made the cover over a five-year period. The last touch was the dead man's pillow, on which he would now rest his head for all eternity.

While the funeral preparations went on, the combined herd was kept together out at Rattlesnake Arroyo under the care and guard of the drovers from the other ranches. All the Circle H Bar cowboys and the other members of the Diablos Range Cattlemen's Association were scheduled to attend Zeb's funeral. The situation at the site of the roundup was still precarious, but at least under control. But things were not so calm that those attending the final services strayed far from their shooting irons. Carbines and revolvers had been left handy in the wagons in case they might be needed in a hurry.

Rawley Pierson, on the other hand, had more than either Zeb's funeral or the trouble with the raiders on his mind. A different situation occupied his thoughts most of the time.

No matter how deep and hidden, all the tenderness and affection Rawley felt for Nancy Hawkins was brought to the surface when he observed her grief at the death of her father.

He could hardly keep himself from going to her side to embrace and hold her as seeing her overwhelming sadness and loss tore at his heart. Rawley experienced no lust for the pretty young woman at that time. Only the deepest caring and sympathy dominated his feelings where Nancy Hawkins was concerned.

By nature, Rawley was an easygoing fellow who took in stride whatever life offered him, be it good luck, danger, or a run of misfortune. Remaining unattached and traveling around with Chaw Stevens was an existence he enjoyed. Something was always happening, even if it was a dreary sheriff's job with occasional outbursts of gunplay, or drudgery on a ranch like the Circle H Bar.

But Rawley felt confusion and worry about his feelings toward Nancy. He'd never felt that way toward a woman before. His limits had been open admiration of a certain female's looks, fleeting affection for a dance-hall girl, or a subtle rejection of a woman he simply didn't like. Women were puzzling things that simply flitted in and out of a fellow's life like bottles of good and bad whiskey. It had all been so simple for him, as uncomplicated as his own life and attitudes.

But now he was as jittery about himself as a puma with a pack of hounds on his tail.

Rawley tried to deny any affection toward Nancy other than as a casual friend, but her distress triggered the deep fondness and caring he truly felt for her. His emotions were so strong that he could not deny even to himself that whatever feelings he had for the young woman ran as broad and deep as the Brazos River. And he was bound and determined to hide those feelings from his best friend.

But old Chaw Stevens, on the other hand, was completely aware of Rawley's true sentiments. The whiskered, bandy-legged codger may have been crude and unlettered, but Chaw was wise far beyond his education. He had a natural, native intelligence that served him well. The Johnny Reb could perceive people in a deep, penetrating manner which had saved his life on several occasions when he'd drawn and fired at some jasper who was shaming a back off during a showdown or arrest. He knew well that Rawley was much taken with Nancy Hawkins. The only thing he wondered about the situation was what those affections might lead to.

The Circle H Bar crew—Rawley, Chaw, Jim Pauley, and Duane Wheeler—dressed in their best clothes on the morning of Zeb Hawkins's funeral. Chaw waited until Jim and Duane had gone outside before he brought up the subject of Nancy Hawkins to Rawley in his usual direct manner.

"Have you gone silly over Miss Nancy?" he asked.

Then he added, "Maybe I should ask *how* silly have you gone over Miss Nancy."

"What?" Rawley asked, looking away from the mirror he was using while brushing back his hair.

"I asked if you'd started liking Miss Nancy a whole lot," Chaw said. He sat on his bunk and struggled into his best boots. They were a nonworking pair he used for special events.

Rawley finished brushing. "Sure I like her. Don't you?"

"Maybe not as much as you," Chaw said.

"Well, that ain't no great surprise. You're a woman-hater," Rawley said with a weak grin. "Ever'body knows that."

"I don't hate 'em exactly," Chaw said. "But I am leery of 'em."

Rawley put on a clean shirt. He eyed his old friend closely. "Now you ain't just jawing up to pass the time before the funeral. Just what're you leading up to?"

"You and me is partners," Chaw said. "So if you're of a mind to settle down, let me know and I can plan on heading out alone after our work here is done."

"Settle down?" Rawley asked.

"Yeah. With Miss Nancy," Chaw said.

Rawley didn't like that particular concern being discussed. "You're loco, Chaw. Sometimes you're as confused as a lost dogie."

"I ain't confused," Chaw said. "But I got no hankering to stay in one place too long. I think maybe you do."

Rawley's thoughts turned to Nancy. Hearing what had been deep in his heart brought out in the open by somebody else made him hesitate before speaking again.

"Well? Are you thinking on staying here or not?" Chaw demanded to know.

74

"Can you leave a feller alone?" Rawley snapped at him. "You're worser than a nagging old grandma!"

Chaw shook his head. "You're thinking on settling down, all right!"

While the two talked in the bunkhouse, Big Ed MacWilliams rolled into the Circle H Bar ranch yard in the livery stable buckboard he'd rented. The big saloon owner drove the vehicle over to one side of the group of horses tied up at the front of the house. After a quick survey of the scene, he stepped out of the small wagon and hobbled the horse.

Fred Blevins stood on the porch. "Howdy, Big Ed."

"Howdy, Fred," Big Ed said, walking up to him. He looked around. "It ain't much of a turnout, is it?"

"It's a shame," Fred said. "In normal times when a man like Zeb Hawkins dies, folks come in droves to pay their last respects. But with a shortage of cowboys and a big herd to be watched, it'll just be his own family and crew along with us other ranchers and our wives."

"These is terrible times on the Diablos, all right," Big Ed said. "I just hope you fellers can either straighten things up or take the chance I offered you to get out smelling perty."

"You know what we're gonna do," Fred said.

"Yeah," Big Ed said. "Well, excuse me, Fred. I'll go pay my respects to the departed and Tim and Miss Nancy." He walked across the porch and went inside the house. The ranchers and their wives were gathered in the living room, drinking coffee that Norma Watkins and Penny Blevins had made for the small crowd.

A coffin, set up on a couple of sawhorses, was situated in front of the fireplace. Big Ed walked over and looked into it. He shook his head. "Poor ol' Zeb."

"He's got kind of a pinched expression on his face," Doak Timmons remarked. "I reckon that comes from

75

getting hit in the chest by a big-caliber bullet."

"I reckon it does," Big Ed agreed. "A feller'd blink mighty hard in a case like that."

"Yeah, he would," Doak said.

Tim Hawkins walked over and offered his hand to Big Ed. "I appreciate you coming out."

"I knowed your pa," Big Ed said. "Maybe I didn't see a lot of him, but I at least wanted to say a last good-bye." He looked around. "Now where might Miss Nancy be? I'd be proud to offer my condolences."

"She's out to the kitchen," Tim said.

Big Ed went through the door, and found Nancy sitting at the table with Myra Timmons and Darlene Lawson. "Good morning, ladies," Big Ed said.

Myra Timmons was a deeply devout woman who insisted that all the cowhands on her husband's Diamond T ranch attend divine services on Sunday morning—hungover or not. She did not approve of Big Ed MacWilliams, his saloon, and especially the women who worked for him. "This is a funeral we're having today, Mister MacWilliams," she said coldly.

"I am painfully aware o' that, Miz Timmons," Big Ed said.

"It is a religious affair in which we'll be offering up prayers for the good of Brother Zeb Hawkins' soul," Myra Timmons said.

"I only wish to bid a mournful farewell to a man I respected and admired so much," Big Ed said. "Surely there ain't no harm in that."

"When the prayers is said, maybe you should listen closely to 'em, Mister MacWilliams," Myra said.

"I promise I will," Big Ed said. He turned to Nancy Hawkins. "I'm terrible, terrible sorry, Miss Nancy."

"Thank you kindly, Mister MacWilliams," Nancy replied softly.

"If there is any service I might do for you, let me

know," Big Ed continued. "There's nothing too much you could ask from me."

Nancy nodded.

"I'd be proud if you'd care to take my arm during the services," Big Ed said.

"I think not," Nancy said. She found the thought of being with Big Ed MacWilliams repugnant. "I have an escort, thank you just the same."

"That's nice," Big Ed remarked. "Your brother no doubt will offer you some degree of comfort during this hard time."

"My escort is not only my brother. I will also be with Mister Rawley Pierson," Nancy said. The words surprised even her, and she didn't know why she'd spoken them.

"Pierson?" Big Ed asked. His face reddened a bit, then he brought his temper under control. "Well. I can see I can't do you much good. At least not today. I'll see you later, Miss Nancy." He walked from the kitchen.

"Are you really going to be on the arm of that handsome Rawley Pierson?" Darlene Lawson asked.

"I just said that," Nancy said. "I didn't want to have to hang on to Mister MacWilliams. This day is bad enough."

"I'll take care of that," Darlene said. She left the table and went out into the living room, going directly up to Tim Hawkins. She whispered in his ear, "You go tell Rawley Pierson he's to escort Nancy with you."

"What?" Tim asked.

"You heard me!" Darlene said. "Do it now."

Tim walked through the group of people and walked outside. He met Rawley and Chaw coming to the house. "Pierson," he said. "You are gonna help me escort my sister at the services."

Rawley was speechless for a moment. "Sure. Be proud to, Tim. I didn't expect that."

"Just do what you're told," Tim said coldly.

The three went into the house. Rawley and Chaw went up to the coffin and stood there for a moment giving Zeb a final, silent farewell. Then they walked over to one side of the room to stand by Jim Pauley and Duane Wheeler.

Doak Timmons, besides running the Diamond T, also acted as a lay preacher on various occasions. He checked his watch. "Well, folks," he announced. "Let's take ol' Zeb up to the burying spot and tend to this sad chore."

Jim Pauley went behind the coffin and lifted the lid he'd made for it. Trying to be as quiet and dignified as possible, he nailed the top shut over the dead man.

Nancy came out of the kitchen with Myra and Darlene. When Tim walked over to her, Rawley followed. The two men flanked her and she slipped her arms into theirs. Rawley felt a thrill at this first touch of the woman who'd caught his fancy.

The pallbearers lifted the coffin and followed Doak out the front door. Rawley, Nancy, and Tim went next, followed by the rest of the people.

The burial place was on a knoll a hundred yards from the main house. There was a gnarled, old cottonwood tree there with a thick trunk and spreading branches that offered a wide shady area on sunny days. Three graves had already been put in on the spot, which was surrounded by a low, wrought-iron fence Zeb Hawkins had ordered from a Pennsylvania company almost fifty years previously.

Two of the people buried in the peaceful spot were Zeb's wives. The third grave was that of an infant child, Nancy and Tim's half-brother, who had succumbed to a summer fever many years before they were born.

The coffin was taken to a freshly dug excavation that Jim Pauley and Duane Wheeler had worked on the previous evening. Using lariats, the pallbearers wasted no time in lowering the coffin containing remains of Zeb Hawkins.

Doak Timmons held his bible as he addressed the mourners. "Folks," he began, "we're all here for the sad task of putting Zeb Hawkins into his final resting place. There ain't nothing too good you can say about a man who left Kentucky and come out West to establish hisself as a honest, hardworking cattle rancher. I can say for sure that Zeb never lied, cheated, nor stole from anybody. He dealt fair and square, giving what he was paid for, and never held a running iron in his hand all the days of his life. Some might think he got a poor reward for being such a good man since he was shot down by masked bushwhackers, but I'd like to remind each and ever' person here that your just rewards don't come to you here on earth—you get 'em in the Kingdom of the Lord. And it comforts me plenty, and I hope it does you too, to know that a good man like Zeb will be sitting pretty up there with the Lord."

Rawley barely paid attention to the words. He was more conscious of feeling pretty Nancy Hawkins's arm on his, the sensation both sweet and sensuous at the same time. He looked over at her, and was surprised to see her looking at him. He smiled and she returned it, sadly, but with the nicest expression in her eyes that Rawley Pierson had ever seen.

Doak continued, "Now let's bow our heads and offer up a prayer for our dear, departed brother." He waited a beat, then said, "Lord, we're sending Zeb Hawkins to you today. He was shot down defending his property from owlhoots who wore masks. Now, Lord, we ain't saying Zeb was perfect, but he sure did a lot more good in this world than bad. He was a Christian and a family man who worked hard, paid out fair, and never put his brand on another man's cow. We're humbly asking you to take him in with you, Lord, and remember that none of us is perfect down here. We ask this in Jesus' name. Amen."

"Amen!" the crowd responded.

Each person, beginning with Zeb's children, picked up a handful of dirt and dropped it in on the coffin. Then the crowd, with the exception of Jim Pauley and Duane Wheeler, who stayed to fill in the grave, walked slowly off the knoll and back to the house.

When they reached the porch, Nancy turned to Rawley. "Thank you for your support, Mister Pierson."

"My pleasure, Miss Nancy."

Chaw stood beside Rawley, watching everyone go into the house to eat the meal prepared by the ranchers' wives. "How come you're standing out here, Rawley? Ain't you hungry?"

Rawley shook his head. "I got some thinking to do."

Chaw patted his shoulder. "You sure as hell do." He took a deep breath. "Well, I'm going in and get some o' them vittles afore they're all gone. I ain't got no romantic thoughts troubling my belly." He cackled. "Losing your appetite is another drawback to being in love."

Rawley turned and walked slowly toward the corral. When he reached it, he climbed up on the fence and settled down on the top rail. His mind deeply occupied, he stared in at the horses inside the enclosure.

Life wasn't so simple and easy anymore.

Chapter 9

After his father's death, Tim Hawkins became the ramrod of the Circle H Bar by both custom and the law of the State of Texas. And true to his arrogant ways, the slim, young man wasted no time in establishing his authority over the ranch's four working cowboys.

He began by meeting his four-man crew in the bunkhouse at wake-up time the day following the funeral. When the drovers rolled out of their blankets, they found the new boss impatiently pacing back and forth. Finally, the rookie ramrod stood by the table in the middle of the bunkhouse, one foot up on a chair as he waited for Rawley, Chaw, Jim, and Duane to pull on their work clothes and boots. After they had dressed, they gathered around their employer.

Duane displayed a lazy smile. "What can we do you for, Tim?"

"The first thing is to stop calling me Tim," the new boss of the ranch said. His face wore a near-sneer. "There's two ways I'm gonna be known on the Circle H Bar. It's gonna be either Mister Hawkins or Boss. Y'all got that?"

Duane, a bit embarrassed and taken aback by the direct snub, was miffed. "Yeah, I reckon."

"That's *yes, sir!*" Tim snapped.

"Yes, sir," Duane said sullenly.

"And you'll do your eating out here like hired help is supposed to do," Tim continued. "No more o' sharing the Hawkins' table. Ever'body got that? Nancy has already been told to serve you off the stove like off a chuck wagon. Then you bring your grub to the bunkhouse or eat it at the corral or wherever you damn well please. But not in the house."

"Say, Boss," Chaw remarked. "Are we gonna still get to use the outhouse behind the barn or do we gotta go out on the prairie somewheres?"

Tim looked directly at the older man. "Is that supposed to be funny?"

"Seems like a reasonable question to me," Chaw said. "Seeing as how there's some rule changes going on around here."

"Well, old-timer, don't worry too much about it, 'cause you're gonna be working them dogies at Rattlesnake Arroyo anyhow 'stead a lazying around the ranch," the youngster said. "So you'll do your business out on the Diablos anyhow. You don't mind pissing on the range, do you?"

"Right now," Chaw said, "there's a couple o' other places I'd like to piss on."

Tim decided to ignore the remark since he wasn't sure what Chaw meant. He glared at Rawley. "You got any questions, Pierson?"

Rawley's eyes glinted with anger and he stared straight at Tim Hawkins. He slowly shook his head, keeping a steady gaze on the new boss. "It's always good for a man to know where he stands."

"You're right about that," Tim said. "I want you in particular to stay in your place."

Jim Pauley said nothing, but the mixed expression of anger and disappointment on his face left no question as to how he felt.

"Let's get on over to the kitchen for your grub," Tim said. "Nancy is gonna give you some tin plates and spoons. Hang on to 'em, 'cause you'll be using them ever' meal. Let's go! There's work to be done!"

Rawley led the way as the cowboys followed Tim out of the bunkhouse and across the ranch yard. They stopped at the back door to the kitchen. Tim went inside to eat as Nancy appeared and began handing out plates heaped with eggs, ham, potatoes, and her good biscuits. It was easy for the crew to tell she wanted to make up for this form of snobbery by giving them extra helpings of her cooking.

"Thank you kindly, Miss Nancy," Rawley said as he took his food.

"I'm real sorry it has to be done this way, Mister Pierson," Nancy said. She looked at the three others. "I apologize."

Chaw was cheerful. "Why, Miss Nancy, I'd stand out under a hot sun on the Staked Plains all of a blazing summer day without no sombrero just to smell that good cooking o' your'n."

She smiled at his crude compliment. "Let's hope this doesn't go on too long."

"And I'd stand in a Montana blizzard on the worstest winter day too," Chaw went on.

"That's enough, Chaw!" Duane snapped. "The rest of us want to eat too."

Nancy went back inside, and returned with tin cups filled to the brim with strong, hot coffee. "There's plenty, so if you want seconds, don't be bashful. Just come on back and knock on the door," Nancy said.

The crew took their breakfasts back to the bunkhouse and settled around the table. They ate hungrily, devouring the delicious food between slurps of coffee.

When Chaw finished, he wiped his mouth. "I been

doing some thinking while taking the wrinkles outta my belly."

"Is that why you didn't do no talking?" Rawley asked. He was used to Chaw keeping a conversation going no matter what.

"That's right," Chaw said looking at him. "And I reached a decision. I'm gonna quit."

"Me too!" Duane Wheeler said.

"And me!" Jim Pauley echoed. "I don't need to be treated like I was a damn farmhand instead of a honest, working cowboy."

"Look, boys," Rawley interjected. "I don't like Tim any better'n you. But we got to stick to this job. At least till the drive to Kansas."

"Oh, yeah?" Chaw asked. "Just tell us why, will you?"

"Out o' respect for the mem'ry of Zeb Hawkins!" Rawley exclaimed. "We all promised him we'd see this thing through. He may be dead, buried, and gone, but the job is still there. We got to stick it out 'cause we give our word to a damn good man. And that includes either making the trail drive to Kansas or die trying like hell to do it."

That made all the sense in the world to the cowboys in the bunkhouse.

"You're right," Duane said. "You don't make a final good-bye to a hell of a man, then forget any deals you made with him."

"I'll make the drive up to Kansas," Chaw said. Then he added, "That is, if'n one o' them masked bushwhackers don't get me first."

The door burst open and Tim Hawkins leaned in. "You've had enough time to eat! Let's saddle up and head out for Rattlesnake Arroyo. *Now!*"

"But this is gonna be trying," Chaw said under his breath as he drank down the last of his coffee.

It took the crew three quarters of an hour before they arrived at the place where the herd was still gathered under the watchful care of the other ranches' cowboys. Rawley and his friends dropped their bedrolls off at the chuck wagon, which was now manned by the cook from the Diamond T. Then they rode out to relieve some of the other drovers so they could come in for eats and a rest.

The day's work was fairly easy but monotonous. The cattle, fattening up on the lush prairie grass, had to be kept in check or they would begin their natural wandering over the wide-open Diablos Range. There was also the possibility of attack, so the cowboys had to be doubly alert, watching animals and the surrounding countryside with equal care. That suspenseful routine would go on for at least another month until the herd was ready for market.

The noises of the day consisted of an occasional moo from a cow and angry shouts from drovers when miscreant cattle disregarded what their human keepers wanted by wandering off. Meadowlarks sang and insects buzzed around under the hot sun. Taking everything into consideration, it wasn't a bad day, except when Tim Hawkins felt like showing off his new position.

The young man shouted unnecessary orders at his drovers throughout the long afternoon, moving them from one place to another for no better reason than to boss them around.

Toward the end of the day, however, that came to a halt when Tim abruptly left the arroyo and galloped away without a word to anybody. Chaw, watching him disappear over the far horizon, chuckled. "That boy's getting to be about as nice to have around as a wildcat with a thorn in its paw."

Rawley displayed a lazy grin. "Yeah! He can sure

brighten a place by just leaving it, can't he?"

While the cowboys continued their work, Tim returned to the ranch and had a hasty supper with Nancy.

"How are the boys doing?" she asked serving him the meal.

"Fine, as long as I keep on their backs," Tim said. "They ain't getting away with nothing as long as I ramrod the Circle H Bar."

Nancy's temper flared up. "Tim! You're acting perfectly awful toward . . ."

He held up his hand. "That's enough, sis! We went through all this early this morning. I'm the boss o' this cattle spread and things are gonna be done my way. Understand? My way!"

"There're two things you're going to have to learn and learn quick," she said. "Gratitude and humility!" Nancy said nothing more. She angrily began to clear the table, working rapidly as she stacked the few dishes on the kitchen counter. She grabbed the bucket from the corner of the room and started for the door to get water to do the washing.

"I'll draw it for you," Tim offered.

"Oh, no!" Nancy snapped. "I wouldn't want anybody as important as you to have to stoop to going to the well."

"Suit yourself!" Tim growled. "I'm going to town anyhow."

Nancy stopped. "To town? Something might happen out there on the range. I think it'd be better, if you didn't stay at the cattle camp, to at least stick to the ranch until after the drive north."

"You do, huh?" Tim said with a laugh.

"I wish you showed as much respect and consideration toward the cowboys as you do that damned Big Ed MacWilliams," Nancy said. "They're more important to the ranch than that saloon keeper."

Tim, ignoring her, went up to his room to change. It didn't take him long to get out of the rough trail clothes into some clean duds. He even traded in his sweat-stained sombrero for a stylish Montana peak that he only wore on special occasions. He avoided seeing Nancy again when he went downstairs to leave.

The ride into town was exhilarating for the young man in spite of having spent the entire day in the saddle. He'd done a good job of hiding the crushing despair he felt at his father's death. Now the prospect of a good poker game, then taking Rosalie or Hannah upstairs, put him in a better mood. He spurred his horse into a canter, traveling down the road that led into Duncan, Texas.

When Tim finally reined up in front of the Deep River Saloon, he found Big Ed MacWilliams in his usual place. The kid unforked the horse and stepped down, walking up to the porch. "Howdy, Big Ed. Y'all got a game going inside?"

Big Ed smiled. "We sure do, Tim. I reckon you're gonna want to make a withdrawal from the bank, ain't you?"

"That's my ammunition," Tim said.

Big Ed got up and beckoned to him. "Well, foller me. You might as well put the boys outta their misery as quick as possible. You do feel lucky, don't you?"

"I reckon," Tim said enthusiastically. A good win at poker would do wonders in wiping away some of the sadness he felt.

They went into the office and Big Ed pulled the money from his safe. He handed it over. "You got over a thousand dollars there now. That's a hell of a grubstake for just about anything a young feller like you might want to do."

"Well," Tim said thoughtfully. "No matter what I

87

end up using it for, I ain't gonna be keeping it in the bank no more. With Pa gone, I'm running things on the Circle H Bar. So I don't have to worry about him finding out about my card-playing and winnings no more."

"You want to sell the place?" Big Ed asked. "I can get you a good price just like I told the other ranchers. As a matter of fact, through an old business partner of mine back East by the name o' Witherspoon, I bet I can get the best price possible for you outta them Eastern fellers."

Tim shook his head. "Nope. Now that I'm in charge, I plan on making the cattle drive to Kansas and coming back with even more dollars to add to this poker money. I'm gonna be the biggest, most powerful rancher on the Diablos."

"Good for you, Tim!" Big Ed said enthusiastically. "Well," he said leading him to the door. "Just jump in that game and wipe 'em out like you always do."

Tim walked over to the table and waited for the hand that was being played to come to an end. Then he bought into the next pot and settled in for some serious card-playing. The hard-eyed saloon girl Hannah O'Dell came around with a bottle of whiskey as always. After pouring everyone a stiff drink, she stood back to watch the action.

The cards were dealt, played, redealt, and replayed. All the familiar games were called out by the dealers: seven-toed Pete, draw, show low, show high, and others. The pasteboards were studied, discarded, and drawn as the players called out bets that were matched or raised. Tim played his usual game, going all out and bluffing like crazy. He didn't give a damn what showed in stud. He stayed with the others to the end of each pot. And he'd call for cards in draw when it looked like he didn't have snowball in hell's chance to pull off a win.

And he lost heavily.

"At last!" Shorty Clemens crowed. "A night that don't belong to Tim Hawkins!"

"The only luck that's shining on me is the bad variety," Tim admitted, the sweat showing on his forehead.

A half hour later, Big Ed MacWilliams came in from the porch. "I hear you're having a rough time."

"I'll get it back," Tim said doggedly. The bad luck reminded him of the loss of his father. He glared at Hank Delong, whose turn it was to deal. "Let's go, goddamn it!"

"Ease off, boy," Big Ed said. "You can't win ever' night."

"The hell I can't!" Tim exclaimed.

On the next hand he won on three of a kind and raked in a modest pot. It put Tim in a better mood. "Now I'm getting it back," he said. He snapped his fingers at Hannah. "Gimme another drink!"

"Sure," she said with a hard smile.

Shorty caught Big Ed's eye and winked. "If this boy gets too mad, we'll all lose big tonight."

"You sure as hell will!" Tim said after downing the liquor. He shoved the glass forward. "Gimme another!"

The other players picked up Tim's sullen mood, and the game settled into a silent affair that was marked only by the clink of coins and the shuffling and dealing of cards. Tim kept losing, and the more he lost, the more he drank.

Finally Big Ed stepped in. "That's enough, boys."

Tim, bleary-eyed, looked up. "I need a chance to get even, that's all."

"Sure, Tim," Big Ed said. "But tonight ain't your night, that's all."

"One more hand, goddamn it!" Tim yelled. "It's my deal."

Big Ed sighed. "Have it your way."

"Ante up for draw poker," Tim said. "One pot, all the same." He shoved all his money in. "No betting after this. I deal the cards and we draw one time only."

Everyone matched him. Shorty Clemens shook his head. "You're loco, Tim."

"Could be," Tim said. He made the deal. "Cards?"

"Gimme two," Shorty said.

"I'll take three," Curly Brandon said. Hank Delong wanted three, and Joe Black decided to take two.

Now Tim studied his own hand. He had a pair of aces, a jack, ten, and a six. He discarded the last three and slapped down their replacements. He had drawn another ace and a pair of threes.

"Nobody calls in this game," Curly said. "So dealer shows first."

Tim grinned. "A full house, boys, aces over threes."

Everyone groaned but Shorty. "Four deuces beats that," he announced.

Tim angrily threw the cards down. He got to his feet and lurched drunkenly toward the door. "I'm going back to the ranch."

Big Ed followed him. "Calm down, Tim," he said when they reached the porch. "There'll be other nights."

"I lost all my other winnings," Tim said. "I'm back where I started."

"Aw, hell, Tim!" Big Ed scoffed. "You're a hell of a poker player. I'll loan you enough to get started again. You'll come back winners again."

Tim felt better. "Damn right I will. And don't you worry one damn bit about any money you loan me."

"O'course I won't. Now come on over to the bar with me and let's have a last drink together before you go back out to the Circle H Bar," Big Ed said.

"Sure!" Tim said happily. As they went back inside, he threw his arm over Big Ed's meaty shoulders. "You know something? You're one o' the best pals I ever had, Big Ed!"

Chapter 10

Out at the cattle camp at Rattlesnake Arroyo, dawn was cool and damp with a heavy dew that clung to the blades of grass in large drops. The sun, coming up slowly over the eastern horizon of the Diablos was sluggish and red, making deep, long shadows in the gullies and among the stands of sagebrush.

The cattle's breath vaporized as the animals waited for the new day to begin. The night before, as planned, they'd been driven into the arroyo so no night raiders could cause a stampede. Packed in tight inside the big gully, the herd took the confinement with numb acceptance.

Rawley Pierson had a Mexican serape over his shoulders as he sat in the saddle looking down at the animals from the rim of the arroyo. It was nearing the end of his turn at the night's final watch. He could smell the smoke from the chuck wagon, and the wafting breeze brought the smell of beans simmering in an iron pot beside the vehicle. At least he could look forward to a brief nap after filling his belly. The last men on guard duty always got an hour's rest before joining the others to begin the day's work.

Chaw Stevens, also sporting a serape, rode toward

him, slouching in the saddle from a combination of sleepiness and boredom. He and Rawley had arranged it so they could always share the same stint of sentry duty. The old man worked the plug in his jaw, enjoying the taste of the tobacco. "Looks like biscuits and beans this morning."

"Yeah," Rawley said. "We have that ever' morning but you act surprised each time."

"I am," Chaw said. "I figger one o' these days that damn cook is gonna serve up something differ'nt."

"Yeah? What do you think it might be?" Rawley asked. "Beans and biscuits 'stead o' biscuits and beans?" He pulled his pocket watch and looked at it. "It'll be time to get the rest o' the boys up in another fifteen minutes."

Chaw took a deep breath. "This is the life, ain't it, Rawley? Away out here in all this clean, fresh air far from some damn stifling town and all the unagreeable folks that live in it." He pointed outward. "Just take a look at this beautiful range country."

"I'll tell you one thing," Rawley said. "I'd rather we was in the town o' Benton so's I could go down to the Blue Bird Cafe for a good breakfast. It'd taste a hell of a lot better'n them damn beans."

"No, it wouldn't," Chaw said. "Food outside is always better 'cause the fresh air gives you an appetite. Anyhow, I reckon you'd prefer to be tasting Miss Nancy's cooking than eat in the best restaurant in Dallas."

"Miss Nancy does a good job on a meal," Rawley said. "Even a damn fool would appreciate that."

"Well, you're a damn fool so you sure as hell oughta know," Chaw said.

"Now what do you mean by that?"

"You had a chance to leave here and you didn't take it. We was all ready to quit yesterday morning, but you talked us into staying on."

"We owe it to Zeb Hawkins," Rawley insisted.

Chaw laughed aloud. "You wanted to stay on at the Circle H Bar on account o' Miss Nancy. And I don't mean just her cooking neither! Now why don't you own up to it?"

Rawley grinned in spite of himself. "Now I'll admit she might've had a little to do with it."

"A little?" Chaw asked laughing again.

"Just shut up," Rawley said. "C'mon. Let's ride on over to the camp and get ever'body up. If it's beans I got to eat, then I want to get it over with as quick as possible."

They rode down to where the other cowboys were wrapped in their blankets. The drovers slept deeply and soundly, as all men do after going to bed following a long, hard day of physical labor.

The cook, stirring his pot by the wagon, looked over at Rawley and Chaw. "Hey," he said. "Hold up waking them fellers. These beans need a little more cooking."

"I doubt if that'd help 'em any," Rawley said.

"Beans is special!" the cook said. "You got to be damn sure ever' time—"

The bullet hit him in the chest, spinning him around and flinging him against the chuck wagon. He bounced off the vehicle, staggering forward, then pitched over dead, hitting the tripod of limbs that held his precious beans over the fire. The cook and his food hit the dirt together.

Rawley and Chaw, still in the saddle, leaped to the ground dragging their carbines with them. More shots splattered into the area. Now working on naked instinct and fear, the rest of the crew had rolled out of their covers. Grabbing their shooting irons, the cowboys fired back in the direction of the incoming bullets.

A group of masked men showed up on the rise to the west of the camp. They turned toward the cowboys and charged down. The drovers turned their guns on them, but more shooting sounded from the north. Another group of the hooded plunderers now came in from that direction.

The camp was caught in a deadly cross fire.

"Get to cover!" Rawley shouted.

The men dove behind anything handy—saddles, bushes, even the chuck wagon—and wasted no time in returning the fire. But the attackers quickly turned off and galloped away.

Others charged in from the south.

One of the Double Box drovers, squatting in the open, was knocked over by a bullet as if a horse had kicked him in the chest. Dying but game, he managed to roll over and get to his knees before falling on his face.

Rawley sized up the situation fast. As an experienced gunfighter, he'd done it all with shooting irons, from an individual showdown to pitched battles on streets and in wide-open country. The raiders were using Indian tactics, hitting at various spots from different angles until they found a weak point to exploit. Rawley damn well knew the best way to handle a situation like that. Don't have any weak points to exploit.

"Hey!" he yelled at the drovers under the chuck wagon. "You want to die there? Get over to the remuda and get saddled up. Me and Chaw can cover these little attacks. And make it pronto!" He knew the small probes were bound to grow larger soon as the attack progressed.

The next assault came from the east on the other side of the arroyo. It would have been impossible for the attackers to cross the gully and charge into the camp, but they peppered the area with several heavy fusillades.

Rawley, picking out one depredator in a large Mexican sombrero, dropped to his knee and took a careful aim. The pull on his carbine trigger was smooth and steady. The weapon kicked back into his shoulder, and the bullet streaked across the open space and smacked straight into the man's face. He was lifted from the saddle and dumped into a heap on the ground. Rawley quickly picked another target, and sent the unfortunate freebooter tumbling into the dust. Now Chaw was firing as quickly and methodically. The bushwhackers wisely pulled back and galloped out of range.

More masked attackers, yelling and firing, came from the west once again. They galloped in closer than before, their ill-aimed but numerous volleys slapping through the area of the cowboy camp.

By then the drovers had saddles across their horses. Sensing that Rawley was in charge, they waited to hear his voice. "Mount up!" Rawley ordered. He pointed to two cowboys near him. "Watch the cattle and keep 'em in the arroyo!" Then he leaped onto his horse and quickly spurred it into a run.

Chaw followed his example, and he was the closest to the impromptu leader as the whole crowd pounded from the camp limits and headed straight at the spoilers.

The gunfire built up into a continuous roar. Two more of the invaders pitched off their mounts and one cowboy went to the ground as the embattled groups closed in. The bushwhackers wisely pulled away as the cowboys came closer. As hired guns, they had no desire to die unnecessarily. The drovers, on the other hand, had a proud, traditional loyalty to their outfits that drove them on into the attack. The code under which they lived and worked demanded loyalty to the ranch straight to the point of death itself if necessary.

When Rawley was convinced they'd driven that particular bunch off, he wheeled his horse to look for another group. It took only a moment before the northern band of outlaws came over the horizon in that direction.

"Hee-yah!" Rawley Pierson bellowed as he led the next attack.

The drovers, wild with excitement now and beginning to feel invincible, quickly galloped after Rawley and Chaw, following the two ex-star-packers' example. The heavier barks of carbine fire intermingled with pistol shots as the charge continued.

This group of attacking outlaws was more stubborn than their other pals. They continued on into the violent onslaught, their own firing doubling as the battlers drew closer across the wide expanse of the Diablos Range. Soon the thundering hooves of all the fighters intermingled to compete with the sound of gunplay.

Duane Wheeler went down as his horse was hit. Flung outward, he flailed in the air until he crashed heavily onto the Texas earth, rolling and bouncing. But he came up on his feet shouting in anger.

His pard Jim Pauley pulled up alongside him. "You hurt, Duane?"

"Just my damn pride!" Duane yelled back. "Wait there a minute." He searched around until he found his carbine. Then, holding onto the Winchester, he scrambled up behind Jim. "Let's go on now!"

The pair, now going slower than the others, nevertheless pushed on to get back into the fight.

The determined cowboys finally broke the spirit of the masked men, who quickly broke away, their formation disintegrating into individuals fleeing for safety. Rawley looked back and saw Chaw close by. He pointed to a pair of the bushwhackers. "Let's get 'em!"

"I'm coming!" Chaw shouted back.

The rest of the drovers also took up individual pursuits. The exceptions were Duane Wheeler and Jim Pauley, riding double, who wisely left the fray to return to the relative safety of the camp. Two men on a horse not only moved slower than hell, but they made a real good target for even a careless shooter.

The two outlaws being chased by Rawley and Chaw rode like hell for a mile before they eased up a bit. But when they noted they were being chased, they spurred their horses to once again begin a mad dash across the wide expanse of Diablos.

Rawley and Chaw, displaying a tenacity built up from their careers as lawmen, pressed on in pursuit. With pistols holstered and carbines in the saddle boots, the pair concentrated only on closing in on their quarry. Now and then, however, they glanced around to make sure no nasty surprises would be sprung on them from other masked outlaws.

The pounding chase continued up rises and down into dips in the countryside, then out once again across the flatlands. The masked men showed a preference to head north, so Rawley and Chaw cut in that direction to force them to veer southward as much as possible. It was a lot like hunting game. Never let your quarry go in the direction it wants to. After a quarter of an hour, all the riders—pursuer and pursued alike—galloped in an easterly route toward the prairie horizon.

The two spoilers drew in close together, shouting to each other. Rawley and Chaw knew what that meant. They went for their guns at about the same time the freebooters reined to a sudden stop and leaped to the ground.

Rawley and Chaw veered off as a brief flurry of shots followed. Within moments, they too were out of the saddle and afoot on the Diablos. The sudden cessation of pounding hooves on the prairie made the range eerily silent to the men who had been going hell-for-leather across the lush grass country only moments before.

"Chaw!" Rawley whispered. "I noticed a draw up there. Them two must've decided to hole up there."

"Yeah," Chaw said. "That's why we can't see the sumbitches now."

"Keep an eye out." Rawley crawled forward a few yards, then suddenly leaped to his feet and ran a few paces before diving down. Several shots burst out. "You see 'em, Chaw?"

"Straight ahead," Chaw responded.

"Cover me!"

Both Rawley and Chaw jumped in. Chaw cut loose with several shots in the direction of the outlaws, while Rawley went forward a distance before flinging himself back into the cover of the grass. They repeated the action, this time with Rawley firing while Chaw maneuvered toward the bushwhackers.

The masked duo was confused by the action. Each time either Rawley or Chaw made a dash, they tried to hit them, but the opportunity for a good shot was too fleeting.

Finally, Rawley had worked himself down into the draw and gone a few yards toward the outlaws. He could easily see both bushwhackers as they strained to catch sight of something to shoot at out on the prairie. Rawley put his carbine in his left hand and drew his Colt. He took a deep breath, then shouted, "Hold there, you two!"

The raiders did not hesitate even a split second before turning toward Rawley with their guns leveled on him. He had no choice but to shoot first and fast. His pistol bucked with each squeeze of the trigger, the bullets flying into the bodies of the hooded desperadoes.

They crumpled under the accurate shooting, dropping to the ground like bags of grain falling from a wagon.

Chaw appeared from the other side. He could see there was no sense in using his own gun. He went to the man nearest him and ripped the hood off. "Here's a stranger."

Rawley took care of the other and saw a familiar face. "Farley Buchanan."

Buchanan wasn't dead yet. Blood came from his nose, mouth, and ears, but he was still conscious. "Howdy, Rawley," he said weakly. "I was right surprised to find it was you when we whipped around there."

"I should've known we'd be seeing you, Farley," Rawley said. "We shot up Jack Freeman a coupla days ago. You and him rode together, didn't you?"

"Hell, yes! Me and him was pards for a long time," Buchanan said. "Was you the one that got him?"

"I don't know," Rawley answered matter-of-factly.

Chaw squatted down beside the fallen gunman. "Howdy, Farley."

"Howdy, Chaw. I got it good, didn't I?"

"You ain't gonna make it," Chaw said bluntly.

Buchanan closed his eyes for a moment, then opened them. "At least it don't hurt much."

"I'm glad o' that, Farley," Rawley said sincerely. "You don't mind telling us who's put you up to this, do you?"

"Are you two packing stars?" Buchanan asked.

Rawley shook his head. "We're working cowboys for one o' the ranches you and your pards keep hitting. And we'd like to know who's paying for your gun."

"I don't know," Farley said. "And even if I did I

wouldn't tell you. I don't give a good goddamn if you're lawmen or not."

"I reckon you don't," Rawley said. "But would you mind telling me the why of it?"

Buchanan groaned. "They want us to run the Diablos clear o' ranchers. That's all I know."

"How's come you don't raid the ranches and burn 'em down?" Chaw asked.

"They don't want the buildings and property ruined," Buchanan replied. He started to speak again, but his breath came up short. "Damn!" He relaxed a moment. "But if I was you fellers I'd get the hell off the Diablos. Whoever wants the range for theirselves has got lots o' money and a strong hankering to own the place."

"Thanks for the warning, Farley," Chaw said.

"You two don't look worried," Buchanan said. He grinned, then the forced smile turned into a grimace. "You winged me once near San Antone, Rawley. So this ain't the first time you shot me, is it?"

Rawley shook his head. "Nope."

"But it's the last," Chaw remarked.

Farley Buchanan grinned again and died.

Chapter 11

The stage driver tugged the reins, bellowing cuss words and loud abuse at the team of horses as the lumbering vehicle left the main trail and rolled over the bumpy prairie toward the nearby town of Duncan. He glanced over at his partner riding shotgun and said, "That uppity sonofabitch is damn lucky I don't throw his ass off right here." He referred to one of the passengers inside. "I should make him walk the rest o' the way and lug that damn suitcase too."

The guard laughed. "Serve him right too for insisting that we take him off the reg'lar route and into town."

"He must think the price of a ticket makes him more powerful than the Almighty," the driver said.

"Them Easterners has got a way about 'em that flat rubs a feller raw, don't they?" the guard complained. "And they talk so damn funny too."

"Gospel truth! Gospel truth!" the driver agreed. "I wonder what brings him out on the Diablos anyhow. This place ain't got shit but stubborn ranchers and bad weather most o' the time."

"Maybe he thinks there's a fancy hotel out here," the guard said.

Five minutes later the stage came to a clattering, squeaking half in front of the most imposing building in the town—the Deep River Saloon. The driver bellowed, "Duncan! Out for Duncan, Texas, on the Diablos Range."

The guard climbed up on the top of the conveyance and grabbed a large, heavy leather suitcase. He heaved it to the ground, where the expensive piece of luggage bounced twice before ending up against the saloon porch.

Calvin Witherspoon stepped from the stage and slammed the door. "Which one of you threw that suitcase to the ground like that?"

"It wasn't me," the driver said. He looked at the guard. "Was it you?"

The guard shook his head. "Nope. It did it on its own."

"That's right," the driver said. "When we come to a stop it hollered out, 'At last!' and jumped right off." He nudged his pal, and they both guffawed and winked at each other.

"Extremely amusing," Witherspoon said. He was a short, dapper man, his expensive suit covered with dust. "You can be assured I shall write your employers about your conduct. You've both been rude and uncaring throughout the entirety of this horrid trip."

"If you think they'll fire us, you're loco, mister," the driver said. "They ain't gonna find nobody else dumb enough like me and Gus to drive out over the Diablos. So long."

"So long!" the guard echoed.

The reins cracked and the horses lurched back into action, going into a wide turn and heading back for the main trail. Witherspoon watched them disappear, then walked up to his suitcase. He wrestled the heavy piece of luggage up on the porch. After catching his breath from the unaccustomed labor, he went to the closed door of the saloon and banged on it.

"MacWilliams!" he yelled out. "Ho, Ed!"

There was no answering sound from inside.

Witherspoon pounded again, frustration and anger making him ignore the pain of hitting the hard door frame. "Ed MacWilliams! Get out here! It's me, Witherspoon!"

A feminine voice, husky with sleep and the previous night's whiskey, called from above. "Who's the noisy sonofabitch down there?"

Witherspoon walked out onto the street so he could look over the roof covering the porch. He could see the unpleasant face of a wasted, faded woman peering down at him. "I'm looking for Ed MacWilliams," he said.

Hannah O'Dell, disheveled and hung over, frowned at him. "Well, he ain't here."

"Then would you mind telling me exactly where in hell he is?" Witherspoon asked in an exasperated tone.

"He's in his room over to the boardinghouse," Hannah said.

Witherspoon clenched his fists in anger at the insolent reaction to his inquiries. "And where might that boardinghouse be, please?"

"It might be in Kansas City, but it ain't," Hannah said with a sneer. "It's over yonder on the other side o' the general store. The only two-story house. Now vamoose so's a lady can get some sleep."

"If there is any lady in there," Witherspoon said coolly, "I hope she was not disturbed."

Hannah laughed. "That's perty good." She slammed the window shut.

Witherspoon started to pick up his suitcase, then

changed his mind. He trudged across the street and walked along the side of the general store, picking his way through the horse droppings and mud puddles. "Oh, God!" he said aloud to himself. "Why did I get myself into a situation where I had to come back to this part of the country?"

The boardinghouse was another twenty yards beyond. He could see a woman sweeping off the front steps of the place. Witherspoon walked up to her and tipped his hat. "Good morning, madam. I'm looking for Ed MacWilliams," he said, expecting the worst.

"Big Ed is in the kitchen having his breakfast," the woman said. "You'll find it in the back of the house."

"Thank you, madam. You are an oasis of kindness and intelligence in this desert of idiocy and impertinence." He went inside, and walked through a parlor until he reached a short hallway. From there he went a short distance until he reached the kitchen. He paused in the door and looked at the large man sitting at the table. "So they call you Big Ed now, do they?"

Big Ed looked up from his plate of eggs, his mouth wide open. "Damn, Cal. I never expected to see you."

"Oh, you really didn't? How strange! You see, that sort of surprises me, Ed. Oh, pardon me! I mean, of course, *Big* Ed. It's just that I figured you'd be expecting to see me or somebody from the way things are going out here."

Big Ed set his fork down. "Let's not start out on the wrong foot again, Cal." He stood up and offered his hand. "I reckon the last time I laid eyes on you, you was a-heading back East right after I bought out your share of our San Angelo bar. You swore you'd never come west o' the Mississippi again."

Witherspoon shook hands with him. "I'm not overly thrilled about being here."

105

"You don't see me dancing the fandango, do you?" Big Ed said. "Living on the Diablos ain't like being in the lap o' luxury."

"Yeah," Witherspoon said. "In your letters you mentioned a string of ill fortune. And that, as you must already have figured out, is exactly what has brought me here."

"A long, long string of bad luck," Big Ed said. "I been run out of a coupla towns and was damn near lynched once."

"You sometimes make very poor judgments and decisions, my old friend," Witherspoon said.

"You don't have to remind me," Big Ed said.

"I need a cup of coffee," Witherspoon said. "I've been on a stage for three days. We either stayed in flea-infested hovels or camped out all night, and traveled as long as there was light enough to see."

Big Ed went to the stove and fetched him some of the hot brew. "It's been a long, long time, Cal. It's just like old times seeing you again. A thousand mem'ries keep jumping into my mind."

"Yeah. We went through our share of adventures— and misadventures—together, didn't we?"

"We sure did," Big Ed answered.

Witherspoon was grateful for the strong coffee. "We got some talking to do."

"This ain't the place to do it," Big Ed said. "Let me finish my grub and we'll go over to the saloon."

"First let me get a room here," Witherspoon said. "I may be forced to stay in town for a bit."

"There ain't a vacancy," Big Ed said. "Some townfolks is here, and a coupla my boys is bunking in one o' the rooms."

"Kick your boys out," Witherspoon said. "I'll take their place."

"Sure, Cal," Big Ed said. "I'll take care of it."

"My suitcase is on the porch of your saloon," Witherspoon continued. "Have someone fetch it to my digs."

"I'll see that it's brung over here," Big Ed promised. "I'll run upstairs and get the fellers up and outta there. Then one of 'em'll fetch your bag for you."

"I'll wait," Witherspoon said.

He could hear Big Ed MacWilliams stomping up the stairs. Within moments there was an angry muttering of masculine voices that quickly quieted down as soon as Big Ed's own voice roared out in instant rage at what he considered insubordination.

Five minutes later, two men carrying saddlebags came down the stairs and went out the front door. Big Ed came back into the kitchen. "It's all set. I'll have Mrs. Malone change the sheets on the bed and clean the room up."

"Good," Witherspoon said.

"You want some breakfast, Cal?" Big Ed asked. "I'll see to that too."

"No, thank you," Witherspoon said. "I am most certainly not hungry after that stage ride. Anyway, I'm anxious for us to have a talk about business."

Big Ed sat back down to finish his eggs. "I sent you a report not more'n a month ago."

"We weren't pleased," Witherspoon said. "In fact, I was under the gun because I'd arranged this whole thing and recommended you personally for the job."

Big Ed pushed his plate away, his face flushed with anger. "Let's get over to my office."

The two walked through the house and went outside, where the boardinghouse's owner, Mrs. Malone, had just finished her sweeping chores. Big Ed nodded to her. "Curly and Joe has moved outta their room, Miz

Malone. My friend Witherspoon is moving in. How about changing the bed and cleaning the place up for him."

"Are you still paying the rent, Mister MacWilliams?" the lady asked.

"Yes, ma'am," Big Ed said.

"You explain my rules to your friend," Mrs. Malone reminded him.

"Don't worry about Mister Witherspoon," Big Ed assured her. "He's a perfect gentleman."

"He looks it," Mrs. Malone said approvingly.

As the two men walked back to the Deep River Saloon, they passed Curly and Joe lugging Witherspoon's heavy suitcase back to the boardinghouse. Curly frowned, saying, "Just where the hell are we supposed to sleep?"

"Yeah," Joe Black said. "There ain't no more rooms in Duncan."

"Move into the saloon, boys," Big Ed told them.

"I take those are the two fellows whose room I'm taking," Witherspoon said.

"That's right," Big Ed said. "But don't worry about it."

"I won't," Witherspoon said flatly.

They paused at the big portal behind the batwing doors as Big Ed opened up the saloon. They went inside, where the stuffy whiskey smell of the previous night's activities hung strong in the air.

"My office is this way," Big Ed said. He grabbed a bottle from the bar as they walked past. "I need an eye-opener."

Witherspoon knew that Big Ed was already wide awake. The liquor was to calm his nerves for what he was about to hear. The office was small and sparsely furnished with a desk, two chairs, and a safe. "This is your headquarters, hey?" Witherspoon remarked.

"What do you expect out here on the Diablos, goddamn it!" Big Ed snapped. "I ain't sitting on my ass in a fancy office back East." He sat down and opened the bottle, immediately treating himself to a couple of deep swallows. "I shoulda gone back with you when you left, I reckon. Want a snort?"

"No, thank you," Witherspoon said. He preferred fine brandy.

"So let's not waste no time. Just haul off and let me know what you and your rich pards in New York is so unhappy about," Big Ed said sullenly. "Maybe it's time for a little old-fashioned Western back talk to bring the facts to you."

"The first thing you do is calm down," Witherspoon said. "I will stand for no browbeating one way or the other."

Big Ed grabbed control of himself. After another drink and a deep breath, he spoke much more calmly. "Have your say."

Witherspoon sat down on the other side of the desk. He pulled a couple of expensive cigars from his jacket pocket. After sliding one over to Big Ed, he lit one for himself. "We want to know what's taking so long."

"It's a tough fight," Big Ed said.

"It's an *expensive* fight," Witherspoon said. "And frankly, we're getting worried about our money. This has turned out to be one hell of an investment. That money might have been better off put into something else. I really need an accounting."

"Well, I sure as hell ain't keeping any books!" Big Ed said. "You want us all to go to jail or the gallows?"

"Let's keep our voices down," Witherspoon warned him. "Now. What's taking so long?"

"These ranchers is tough," Big Ed said. "I told you

that when you and your syndicate decided you wanted the Diablos."

"And we gave you enough money to finance a large gang," Witherspoon said. "As I recall, one of your messages indicated you had as many as twenty-five hired guns."

"I did," Big Ed said. "But now there's a hell of a lot less. A bunch has been shot up, and a lot has quit saying the pay ain't worth the risk."

"But the ranchers were losing cowboys long before this," Witherspoon said. "What's happened?"

"Two things," Big Ed said. "First, the ranchers formed up a cattlemen's association under Zeb Hawkins, who has always been kind of a leader out here. When he got kilt, I figgered that the association would dry up and go away."

"What happened?"

"Two tough hombres—or I should say, one tough hombre with a sidekick—has come onto the Diablos," Big Ed said. "I found out they was lawmen down in Benton to the south. They're damn good with their irons, and ever'body is willing put up a stiff fight as long as they're around."

"Who is this spectacular fellow?" Witherspoon asked.

"His name is Rawley Pierson," Big Ed said.

"Then, my old friend, we should see that this Mister Rawley Pierson is done away with as quickly as possible," Witherspoon said.

"He's been shot at in raids, but we ain't got him yet," Big Ed said. He liked the idea of concentrating on getting rid of Rawley Pierson. Not only would it remove a big stumbling block in the scheme to grab control of the Diablos, but his rival for Nancy Hawkins's affections would also be gone for good.

"Then send some of your boys out after him personally," Witherspoon said. "Their only job will be to shoot this bothersome fellow."

"You mean forget the plan and the ranches and the cattle till we get him?" Big Ed asked. He smiled. "By God, Cal! I think that's a hell of a fine idea."

"Of course it is," Witherspoon said.

"Now let me pass on some more information to you, so you don't think I been laying down on the job here," Big Ed said.

"I'm anxious to hear something positive," Witherspoon said with a tone of relief in his voice.

"We got the sheriff on our side," Big Ed said. "Fact o' the matter, he's come in handy on a coupla occasions when the law was asked in on the raids."

Witherspoon smiled. "Now that *is* good news."

"There's something better," Big Ed said, leaning forward. "One o' the ranchers' sons is in my hip pocket. Since his pa got killed he's ramrodding his outfit."

"How can you control him?" Witherspoon asked.

"A great big poker debt," Big Ed replied. "And he thinks I'm one of his best pals."

Witherspoon winked at his old partner. "Now that's the Ed MacWilliams I know."

"I thought that'd make you grin," Big Ed said.

"Speaking of the ranches out on the range, just what is the situation out there right now?"

"The cattlemen are fattening up their herds for the drive up to Kansas in about a month," Big Ed answered.

"Is there anyone left in that intrepid army of yours that can take this Rawley Pierson?" Witherspoon asked.

"Sure. Walt Deacon is the feller's name," Big Ed answered. "But he'll have to be sneaky about it. Prob'ly

111

have to backshoot him. That's 'cause he ain't as fast as Rawley. But he can shoot the eyebrows off a hummingbird at a hunnerd yards—and that's with a pistol. He's even better with a rifle."

"Then, Ed," Witherspoon said slowly and deliberately, "get the word out to Walt Deacon to take his best rifle and go shoot Pierson in the back when he's not looking."

"I'll take care of that right away," Big Ed said.

Chapter 12

Nancy Hawkins felt the twinge of a headache as she labored on the task of bringing the account books up to date. She had duly noted all salaries paid out, the purchase of leather harnesses, having a couple of horses from the remuda reshod, and other business expenses that had either been paid or put on account for the Circle H Bar ranch in its hectic activities to prepare for the cattle drive to Kansas.

She sighed as she closed the volume, knowing that the difference between prosperity and a terribly bad year that could easily include the loss of the ranch depended on that scheduled drive to the north. The young woman got up from the desk in the little room just off the parlor that served as the ranch's business office. She walked through the house, still feeling that pounding in her temples after going through all the adding and subtracting. The task of checking the figures had been both tiresome and worrisome. She'd begun the work early in the morning, and it was now noon. To add to her discomfiture, Nancy hadn't been at all pleased with what she'd found where her brother Tim was concerned.

She paused at the mantel long enough to look at the photo of her father and his first wife. She regretted that a later one had never been taken. It would have been nice to be able to remember him as he was in the fullness of life, rather than as a corpse shot down by some coward wearing a mask. But there was no photographer in Duncan, and no itinerant cameraman had ever shown up to ply his trade on the Diablos. Neither she nor Tim had ever had the opportunity to get their own pictures taken.

The sound of a horse drawing up outside caught her attention. Nancy got the Colt .44 pistol off the side table and cautiously looked outside. She relaxed when she saw it was Tim returning from the herd at Rattlesnake Arroyo.

She put the pistol back and waited for him to come in. When he walked into the house, dusty and sweaty, she treated him to a faint smile. "It looks like you've had a busy time of it."

"I sure have," he answered. "Some o' the Diamond T cattle found their way outta the arroyo just after dawn. We had a real job chasing 'em down." He slapped at the dust on his trousers. "What makes it take so damn much time is having to keep one eye out for masked hombres and the other on the cattle."

"Has that been the only trouble you had out there lately?" she asked.

"Yeah. It's been so quiet that we've decided to send some fellers back to the ranches to tend to chores that's been neglected," Tim explained. "Rawley Pierson is gonna come in to mend that corral fence this afternoon."

"Are you going to help him?"

Tim shook his head. "Nope. I'm taking advantage of the time off to go into town."

114

"I don't think that's a good idea, Tim," Nancy said.

"You've been saying that a lot lately," he said testily. "And I'm getting tired of it."

"I've an especially good reason to say so now," Nancy said.

"And what might that be?"

"Are you gambling?" she asked in a direct manner.

"What's the matter?"

"I've just finished balancing the books, and I see you've pulled some cash out of the operating funds," Nancy said. "And no expenditures have been made with them. At least none are listed."

"So what? I ain't making a secret of it," Tim said with a shrug.

"We need all our money to keep going until that cattle drive," Nancy said.

"Yeah, I know," Tim said. "But maybe I figgered out a way to make it grow some between now and when we move them cattle to Kansas."

Nancy pursed her lips. "You *are* gambling!"

"The way I play poker, sister, it ain't gambling," Tim said. "I've been cleaning them boys out in the Deep River Saloon perty reg'lar."

"Then where're your winnings?" Nancy asked.

"I hit a bad streak o' luck, but it's due to fade away anytime," Tim said confidently. "I can feel it in my bones."

"And you're drinking heavier than ever," Nancy said. "During the last raid on the camp out at the arroyo, you were sleeping off a drunk right here in bed while our own hands and the men from the other ranches did the fighting."

"I can't be out there all the time!" Tim snapped. "And how'm I supposed to know when we're gonna get hit out there? Anyhow, the boys handled it just fine." He

115

changed the subject. "Is there a fire in the stove? I want to heat some water for a bath."

"Help yourself," Nancy said coldly.

Tim immediately put her protests and arguments out of his mind as he went upstairs to fetch a change of clothing. When he returned to the kitchen, he fixed up a tubful of hot water and climbed into it. After cheerfully scrubbing the range sweat and dirt off, he got out and toweled himself dry. The next chore was to get into fresh clothing for an immediate trip to town. He figured if he got an earlier than usual start, he would have more time to begin turning things around in his efforts at poker.

His luck had remained bad for the past week. He owed Big Ed MacWilliams a big pile of money—over five hundred dollars—but Tim knew that one or two good evenings would not only square the debt, but give him a healthy profit too. Since Big Ed seemed cheerfully willing to advance him the funds, Tim's optimism remained high. After all, Big Ed wouldn't back somebody he'd figure as a loser.

After Tim had prepared himself he left the kitchen, and found Nancy sitting in a rocker on the porch. He looked down at his sister. "Don't worry. Maybe tonight is the night I'll come back with enough money so we can run this ranch for the next five years without worrying."

Nancy said nothing. She watched him mount up and ride out of the ranch yard. When he looked back and waved, she made no move. Tim disappeared from sight, and the young woman stood there for a long time, lost in worried thought.

"Miss Nancy." Rawley Pierson's voice broke into her reverie.

She looked over at the side of the porch and saw him

dismounting. She found the sight of the handsome man extremely pleasant. "Hello, Mister Pierson. I haven't seen you for a while."

"We've kept busy out at the arroyo," Rawley said, walking up to her. "The boss wanted me to come in and fix that corral fence."

"The boss!" she exclaimed. "Does he insist you call him that?"

"That he does," Rawley said. "It's all right. We don't mind. After all, that's what he is."

"Papa was never called anything but his name," Nancy said.

"Differ'nt folks use differ'nt styles," Rawley pointed out. "Well, I reckon I'll get to work. Tim says the tools are in the barn."

"Yes," Nancy said. "They're kept with the extra harnesses in the far corner."

"It's nice seeing you again," Rawley said. "We miss your cooking."

Nancy laughed. "I've heard about the new cook. Tim says he's even worse than the old one."

"He sure is," Rawley said. "Chaw says we could grind his biscuits down to bullets if we'd a mind to do so."

"How is old Chaw? It's not the same around here without his complaining," Nancy said.

"Believe me, we get enough of that out there," Rawley said. "Well, I'd best to get work."

He left her and walked out to the barn. The hammer and nails were on a shelf beneath the pegs holding harnesses and bridles. Some extra planking, weather-worn but sturdy, was also there. Rawley grabbed an armful of what he needed and lugged the load out to the corral.

Rawley wasted no time in getting to work. First he

inspected the fence and did some renailing where that would help. After that, the cowboy pulled off broken boards and those that were split so bad that it wouldn't take much force from some rambunctious bronco to knock them loose.

That was the most difficult part of the chore. Prying and tugging, he worked hard wrestling the stubborn slabs of wood from where they'd been solidly attached to the four-by-four posts sunk in the ground. Once that was done, Rawley settled in to replacing them with newer boards, nailing them solidly to the supports that made up the framework of the big fence.

He was almost two hours into the chore when Nancy interrupted him with some fresh, cool well water. "You look like a thirsty man," she said.

"I sure am," he said gratefully, taking a glassful. He drank it. "I got to admit that there's times when water tastes better'n beer. And this is one o' them times."

"I can imagine," Nancy said, noting how hot the afternoon had become.

Rawley consumed three glasses before his thirst was slaked. "I thank you kindly, Miss Nancy."

"I hope you're planning on staying for supper," Nancy said.

"I'd truly like to," Rawley said. "But I reckon the boss is gonna want me to get back to the herd as quick as possible when I finish with the corral."

"I don't care what Tim wants," Nancy said drily. "I'll be planning on you eating with us. And that means in the kitchen. Not out in the bunkhouse."

"That's most kind o' you," Rawley said. "But I don't want to be the cause of any trouble between you and your brother."

"You don't have to worry about that, Mister Pierson," Nancy assured him.

118

"In that case, it will be my pleasure, Miss Nancy," Rawley remarked.

She left him, and went to the smoke house to select a ham to bake that night. As she walked back to the kitchen with the meat, she glanced over at Rawley. He seemed the most handsome man she'd ever seen in her life. Nancy recalled that he was particularly fond of her buttermilk biscuits, so she decided to prepare a batch for supper.

Rawley wasn't so sure if staying over to eat at the ranch was such a good idea. No matter what Nancy said, there was no doubt that the situation would not be a welcome one for Tim Hawkins. Rawley knew that in spite of the fact that Nancy had insisted he stay, the young rancher would go out of his way to make things unpleasant out on the Diablos. And Rawley knew that sooner or later he'd finally lose his temper and dust the boss's nose with his fist. Not that he'd regret it, but it would mean he would have to leave the ranch. And that meant leaving Nancy too.

But by the time he'd finished his chore and Nancy came out to fetch him to eat, Tim had not returned from town. Grateful for the slight chance of a reprieve, Rawley washed up and went inside the kitchen.

"Tim hasn't shown up yet, hey?" he remarked.

"I really don't expect him, Mister Pierson," Nancy said. She pulled the pan of biscuits out of the oven.

Rawley sniffed the air. "Buttermilk biscuits!"

"Oh? Are you fond of them?" Nancy asked innocently.

"I sure am, Miss Nancy," Rawley said. "And I never tasted none better'n yours."

"Sit down," Nancy said. "We can eat now." They settled themselves around the table. Then she asked, "Will you say grace, Mister Pierson?"

Rawley smiled apologetically. "I'm right sorry, Miss Nancy. But I don't know any prayers."

"All you need do is bow your head and say, 'Thank you, Lord, for this food. Amen.' It's real easy," Nancy explained.

Rawley bowed his head. "Thank you, Lord, for this grub—I mean food. Amen."

"That is a habit you should get used to," Nancy said softly. "Will you carve the ham, Mister Pierson?"

"Sure!"

They ate slowly and with much enjoyment, as much for being in each other's company as for the good food. Their conversation was light and sparkled with laughter as good humor eased into the lightness of the meal's mood. Rawley had plenty of stories about himself and Chaw beginning when he was a boy and going right up to when they worked as lawmen together down in southern Texas.

When supper was finished, Rawley got up and helped Nancy clear the table. He even went outside and drew water to do the dishes. While she washed the utensils, Rawley made himself useful by cleaning the ashes from the stove and laying the fire for the next morning. A half hour after they'd finished eating, the couple stood in a clean kitchen with everything put away in its proper place.

"I reckon I'd better get back out to the herd, Miss Nancy," Rawley said. "And I thank you most kindly for the nice supper and your hospitality."

"Why don't I slice some ham and you can take it out to Chaw and the boys," Nancy suggested. "After the way you described the food you're eating out there, I'm sure they'd appreciate it."

"They sure will!" Rawley agreed with a laugh.

Nancy started to walk in front of him to get to the

kitchen counter. Rawley, impulsively without thinking, reached out and took her arm. He immediately let her go and started to apologize, but Nancy turned and moved close to him. They embraced, and Rawley gently kissed her when she raised her face to his.

"I was only staying here on account o' you," Rawley blurted out.

"I'm happy to hear that," Nancy said.

He kissed her again. This time longer, and she hugged him tightly around the neck. The situation that had developed between the two was not a trivial fancy. A Texas woman did not allow herself to be kissed by a man unless she was extremely fond of him. And a self-respecting Texas man did not try to kiss a decent woman unless he was prepared to be nothing but honorable with her. What they had done, as far as both were concerned, was to declare their love for each other.

"I don't want to spoil the nice way we feel, but I wonder what Tim's gonna say when we tell him," Rawley said.

"I don't really care, Mister—" She laughed. "Rawley!"

"Nancy!"

"It's about time we called each other by our first names," Nancy said.

Rawley grinned. "I reckon."

"Tim will have to take things as they are," Nancy said. "But let me tell him."

"But I'll have to do the asking for your hand," Rawley reminded her.

"Of course," Nancy said. She stepped back. "Now let me get that ham."

Rawley waited until she'd cut and wrapped a few slices. She even put in some buttermilk biscuits,

121

although there was only enough to give Chaw, Jim Pauley, and Duane Wheeler one each. Rawley had gobbled down a good share of them during supper.

Nancy handed the food to Rawley. "I wish you didn't have to go."

"Me too," he said sincerely. "But we can't stay shorthanded for long out there." He kissed her again. "I'll see you first chance, Nancy."

"We won't have all the time we want together until after the cattle drive," Nancy said.

Rawley nodded. "That's when our lives are gonna change a whole lot. When we get back from Kansas."

"We must be patient until then," Nancy said.

"We got a lotta plans to make," Rawley reminded her.

She nodded, and walked him out the door to his horse. One more kiss, and Rawley mounted to ride slowly out of the ranch yard. He paused at the gate to wave back to Nancy, then headed out onto the Diablos.

Nancy stood there long enough to watch him ride into the growing gloom of evening. Then she turned and walked back to the house, feeling both happy and sad at the same time. She was glad the man she loved returned her affections, but sad that they couldn't spend more time together.

Nancy went to the parlor and lit a lamp, turning it up enough to read. She had a copy of a romantic novel she'd purchased from a traveling salesman passing through more than a year previously. She'd considered the book silly before, but now was in the mood to read about a love affair.

She wasn't sure how long she'd sat there, lost in the book, when the sound of Tim riding up interrupted her. She went outside to meet him. The sight of her brother wasn't at all pleasing to the young woman.

Tim sat reeling in the saddle, his mood black. "My goddamned luck has stayed rotten," he said. He slipped from the horse's back, and almost fell before reaching the ground. Lurching and reeling, he got up on the porch and staggered past Nancy to go into the house.

Nancy stood there for a while, then went back into the house and picked up the lantern. She had to see to putting the irresponsible young man's horse away in the barn for the night.

Chapter 13

Chaw Stevens rode silently alongside his partner, Rawley Pierson, glancing at him from time to time. The older man thoughtfully chewed on the wad of tobacco in his jaw as he pondered the current situation in his mind.

They moved slowly along the top of Rattlesnake Arroyo, watching the cattle grazing in the large gully. Rawley couldn't help but notice he was under some kind of scrutiny, but each time he tried to catch Chaw's eye, the ex-Johnny Reb would quickly look away.

Finally tiring of the game, Rawley urged his horse next to Chaw's. "What's on your mind?"

"Huh?" Chaw replied with what he considered an expression of complete innocence on his whiskery, grizzled old face. "Now what makes you think I got something on my mind?"

"Don't act so all-fired smart. You got a burr under your saddle," Rawley said. "Let's get it out and maybe you'll feel better."

"Well," Chaw said slowly. "I was just wondering about something, that's all."

"Yeah?" Rawley remarked. "That ain't hard to figger out. But what do you got flitting through your mind?"

"Well," Chaw repeated slowly again. "I was just wondering about what's gonna happen after the cattle drive up north to Kansas."

"What about it?"

"Well—"

"If you say that one more time I'm gonna stop talking to you," Rawley threatened.

"I was wondering if I'd be going down to Delbert's place alone after the cattle drive," Chaw said rapidly. "What I need to know is if you're coming back here to the Diablos and the Circle H Bar."

Rawley grinned, enjoying the chance to tease his old pal. "Why, Chaw. What makes you think I'd come back here to this particular range?"

"On account o' when you went back to *fix* that corral yesterday, you was gone long enough to *build* a dozen new ones," Chaw said. "Then you bring that ham and biscuits back with you. I might add that them was buttermilk biscuits."

"So what?" Rawley asked.

"I figger Miss Nancy went outta her way on account o' it was you that went back to work on the ranch," Chaw said.

"That don't mean nothing," Rawley said, enjoying himself.

"And you had a real dumb look on your face too," Chaw said accusingly. "Fact o' the matter is, you look kinda dumb right now."

"Maybe I've always looked kinda dumb."

"I gotta admit you're right about that!" Chaw spat a stream of tobacco juice. "But this time it's a differ'nt kinda dumbness with a lotta stupid grinning. Now tell me straight out—have you and Miss Nancy come to a understanding?"

Rawley nodded. "I reckon I gotta tell you. Yeah. We're intending for each other."

Chaw nodded, then smiled and offered his hand. "I'm glad to finally see it happen. Best wishes for a good life from your old pard here."

Rawley shook his hand. "Thanks, Chaw. I didn't know if you'd approve or not."

"Damnation, yes, I approve!" Chaw said. "Just 'cause I ain't the marrying kind never meant I figgered it best for you. She's a fine young woman—though I'd prefer a nice, broke-in widder myself if I was to hitch up with a gal—and I know you two is gonna do fine together." He paused. "But I think you'd better plan on starting your own spread. I don't think the Circle H Bar is gonna be the place for either of you."

"Why not?" Rawley asked.

"On account o' here comes Tim Hawkins riding over here and he looks as riled as a puma with his tail caught in a barbed-wire fence."

Rawley turned and looked to see Tim galloping toward them. From the way Tim whipped his reins, it was easy to see he was in a bad temper. The young man drew up his horse in a cloud of dust and shower of dirt clods.

"Goddamn you, Pierson! You son of a bitch!"

Rawley's hand dropped to his pistol handle, but he controlled his raging temper. "I've shot men for that," he said coldly. "And I'm at the point where I'm telling you now. Watch how you speak to me."

"You stay away from my sister!" Tim snarled.

"Did she tell you to tell me that?" Rawley asked, knowing then that Nancy had undoubtedly let the young man know of their romance.

Tim unbuckled his gunbelt and wrapped it around the saddle horn. "This is something where a no-good bastard gets a beating instead o' shot like a man."

"You're loco, boy!" Chaw said. "Why don't you just calm down and back off before—"

126

"Shut your mouth!" Tim shouted, sliding from the saddle. "All right, Pierson. I'm unarmed and ready to go toe-to-toe with you."

Rawley smiled grimly. "This is something I been kinda looking forward to." He removed his own pistol belt and draped it across his saddle. In spite of Tim's wild anger, Rawley knew the young man wouldn't draw on him. He stepped out of the stirrups and approached his raging opponent.

Tim cut loose with a wild, swinging right that Rawley stepped inside of. He peppered the young man with a couple of quick lefts, then plowed a straight jab into his jaw.

Tim went down, rolled over on his back, and was back on his feet in a fury. There was no doubt he was Zeb Hawkins's son. A smack to the face wasn't going to slow him down one bit. Tim attacked ferociously, throwing rapid punches that made Rawley backpedal into a defensive posture.

Rawley hunched his muscular shoulders and traded punches, finding some satisfaction in landing a few, but catching some hard blows on both sides of his face. Tim was a slim young man without a lot of weight, but he was fast and possessed a whiplike strength in his arms that drove his fists hard and true. Add that to pure guts and natural-born grit, and he was one hell of an opponent.

Chaw had quickly dismounted and gathered up the reins of his own horse as well as those of the struggling combatants. He held onto the animals, controlling them as best he could while watching the raging fisticuffs that ranged back and forth on the arroyo rim.

Tim slipped in an uppercut that rocked Rawley's head back. Dizzy and a bit nauseous, the cowboy slugged back instinctively as his mind cleared from the heavy punch. A couple of rapid punches snapped

127

Rawley's head around some more and his vision blurred. Now knowing that Tim had a natural talent as a fistfighter, he moved in closer to keep the rancher's ability to maneuver to a minimum.

The two grasped at each other, continuing their pummeling until, completely caught up in the fight, they stumbled over the edge of the arroyo and fell down the side. Rolling, punching, kicking, cussing, and snarling, the two fighters hit the bottom. The nearest cattle, curious but wary, pulled back a bit as the two men struggled to their feet and went back to trading rapid punches.

Their faces were bruised and badly pummeled by each other's gloved hands. The heavy leather gloves with scuffed surfaces caused abrasions on their cheeks under the eyes. Neither noticed the pain as their rage and determination built up. Bleeding, sweat-soaked, and panting, the pair slammed and smashed each other for another full ten minutes.

Finally, their strength began waning from the extreme effort. Jim Pauley and Duane Wheeler joined Chaw on top of the gully. The trio watched as both Rawley and Tim fought like staggering, drunken men, their legs watery and wavering. Then there was a lapse of time between the flurries of blows.

Chaw handed the reins of the three horses over to Duane. "Hang on to these. I reckon the time's come when that fight can be broke up."

The old man got his canteen, then carefully kept his balance as he slipped and slid to the arroyo floor. He walked up to the exhausted combatants and stepped between them. "I reckon it's over."

Tim, bleeding and still furious but almost without energy, stood wavering. "Oh—no—it—ain't—"

"Yeah. It is," Chaw said. He gave him a gentle push, and Tim collapsed to the dirt. He turned to Rawley, grabbing his shoulders and sitting him down. Rawley, no matter how hard he tried, couldn't move against Chaw's strength.

"Now," the old man said. "You both just sit there for a bit." He looked up at Duane. "Go over to the chuck wagon and fetch some o' that liniment they got for medicine. These boys want a little doctoring."

Rawley tried to get up, but couldn't manage it. He settled back, keeping a wary eye on Tim, who now stared at the ground in exhausted bewilderment.

Chaw gave them each a drink of water, then splashed some of the canteen's contents on their faces. "Well now, I reckon all this has been brought out and dealt with." He turned to Tim. "Now if you ain't total blind and stupid, you must know that Miss Nancy has took a real fancy to Rawley. And Rawley has returned them affections in a most honorable way. You ain't got no reason to kick up a ruckus over something like that when ever'thing is decent and above board."

"I don't like him," Tim murmured.

"Hell! He don't like you neither," Chaw said. "But he ain't getting hitched to you, is he? And as far as I been able to determine, Miss Nancy is of a age where she don't need no permission from you."

Rawley finally got to his feet. "Now looky here, Tim. What Chaw said is right. I'm obliged by a personal promise to your pa to help get them cattle to Kansas. I have also made my feelings for Nancy known to her and she said that's fine by her. I'm gonna marry her."

Now Tim got to his feet, but he showed no inclination to continue the fight. "Oh, you are, huh?"

"Yeah! We'll leave the Circle H Bar and live somewhere else," Rawley said. "It's your ranch and I'll respect that. Now if you want me off this cattle drive, just say so and I'm gone. But I'm taking Nancy with me."

By now Tim's head was clear. He knew that if Rawley left, so would the other Circle H Bar hands. Even being addle-brained from a lot of punches, he didn't fool himself into thinking the hands were loyal to *him*. "We got to get them cattle to market," he said. "I owe that to my pa too. But after we reach Kansas, I'm paying you off, Rawley Pierson."

"Good enough," Rawley said.

Chaw then showed some of the instinctive intelligence and savvy he had. "I reckon this'd be a good time for Rawley to ride the south circuit for a while. You two should stay outta each other's way for the rest o' the day."

Tim nodded. Duane came back with the liniment. After Chaw applied the stinging stuff to cuts and abrasions, Rawley and Tim struggled back up to the top of the arroyo, where their horses were tended to by Jim Pauley. Rawley, wasting no time, quickly mounted up and rode off toward the south to the lookout area set up on that side of the cattle camp.

It took him more than a quarter of an hour to reach the spot, which was the highest stretch of land on the Diablos Range. It was a ridge of sorts that rose out of the prairie to a point where it was six feet higher than the surrounding terrain. It ran for almost three miles before sinking down once again into the flatness of the rest of the countryside.

Rawley could see for miles in all directions. The deep buffalo grass seemed almost like an ocean as the wind wafted over it, making the tall blades move back and forth in patterns that stretched to each far horizon. The sky, as always in the plains country, seemed larger and wider than anyplace else in the world. A sweet smell from blooming plants also came on the breeze. Rawley, his face aching and burning from the fight and liniment, slowly began to feel a bit better and more at peace with himself and the world.

He felt the hard blow to his shoulder that knocked him from his horse before he heard the distant shot of the rifle.

A little over three hundred yards away, a hired gun named Walt Deacon lowered his Winchester .44-.40 rifle and smiled to himself. He'd been tracking Rawley Pierson most of the day after spending the previous one waiting for him to show up at the cattle camp. He didn't know what the fight was about that took Rawley tumbling down into the arroyo, but he was glad when it was over and the tall man finally rode out into the open where he could trail him to a good spot for a killing shot.

Curly Brandon had promised him one hundred dollars cash money for the killing of Rawley Pierson. Walt Deacon had thought it funny to be paid for something he'd gladly have done on his own for the pure pleasure of it. Rawley owed him plenty after an arrest and conviction in Benton that had cost him five years of his life in the state penitentiary.

Still grinning, Deacon swung up into his saddle and rode his horse over to where Rawley Pierson's mount still stood on the high ground that had made him such a good target. Deacon reached the horse and dismounted, walking around to finish off the job. Then he froze in confused fear. Rawley was nowhere in sight.

"Hold it, Walt, goddamn your eyes!"

Deacon froze, an ice-cold stab of fear and anger coursing through him. He said nothing as he heard the scuffling footsteps coming up from the small draw below the ridge.

"Drop that rifle *now!*" It was Rawley's voice.

Deacon wisely did as he was told, and turned around slowly when ordered to do so.

Rawley Pierson, his shoulder bleeding, stood there

131

with his Colt drawn. His face was ashen under the bruises there. "You was always a backshooter, wasn't you?"

Deacon said nothing, but instinctively stepped back from the sight of the man he'd just tried to murder.

"I'm taking you back to the camp for a little talk, Walt," Rawley said. "Don't as much as blink a sneaky eye while I mount up. You got a hell of a walk ahead o' you."

Deacon's mind raced with numerous thoughts. He knew what his fate would be out on that lonely range. After a good beating to find out who'd put him up to the ambush, the cowboys would merrily string him up without so much as another howdy-do.

"Turn around and face the north," Rawley said.

Deacon slowly turned, then went for his pistol, whipping the rest of the way around to face Rawley. He had the Remington halfway out of the holster when Rawley's bullet hit him just under the chest and staggered him backward. He went to the ground flat on his back, hitting so hard that he loudly grunted. Deacon grimaced and tried to sit up. The second bullet smashed through his teeth and bounced off the back of his skull before blasting out the top of his head.

Rawley, sore and bleeding, looked down at the dead man. He reholstered his Colt and sighed. "This just ain't been my day."

Chapter 14

The strike of the heavy rifle bullet into Rawley Pierson's right shoulder had broken no bones, but the wound it caused was extremely painful. A hunk of flesh had been gouged out by the .44-.40 slug, and the cowboy found it difficult to move that arm. He also had a blackened eye and swollen nose from the fistfight with Tim Hawkins.

Duane Wheeler observed his condition with typical cowpoke sympathy. "But God, Rawley, you got the looks of a feller that thought the other feller said *stand up* when he really said *shut up.*"

Rawley grinned at that one.

Chaw, with plenty of experience in gunshot wounds, saw to the cleaning and dressing of the injury, kneeling beside his partner, who squatted patiently and quietly throughout the painful treatment. Chaw felt it necessary to explain to Rawley what he could see. "You're all tore up and bruised where the bullet smacked you and went in, so's you'll be pained after a while."

"I'm pained now," Rawley said calmly.

"It'll hurt more later," Chaw promised.

Although the initial bleeding had been a bit heavy, it had quickly tapered off since no arteries were hit. Chaw bound up the shoulder, then fashioned a sling for the right arm to avoid any unnecessary movement that might open the wound and slow down the healing process.

"You keep that wing bound up, boy," Chaw advised him. "I'm more worried about infection than anything else. Anyhow, you ain't gonna be worth much out here for a while."

"I can ride," Rawley said.

Tim Hawkins, his face as battered as Rawley's, offered no sympathy. "You can stick in close to the arroyo and keep an eye out for trouble."

The body of Walt Deacon, laboriously and painfully slung over his horse by Rawley, was searched for any clues as to who might have put him up to the deed.

"You say you knowed this jasper before and even arrested him once," Fred Blevins of the Double Box said. "Maybe he wanted to get even with you."

"There was bad blood between us, all right," Rawley admitted as he adjusted his arm in the sling.

"Yeah," Chaw said. "But I don't think he'd trail us all the way up here just for that."

"He didn't have a mask," Ted Lawson of the Flying Heart said. "We don't even know if he was one o' the bunch that's been raiding us."

"He hires hisself out for mischief," Chaw said. "And he's been on both sides o' the law. Trouble with Walt Deacon is that he's tempted by money. He'd guard your cattle till death did him part unless another feller offered him a cut for helping to rustle 'em."

A call came from the lookout to the west. "Riders a-coming in!"

The group waited while two horsemen approached slowly and carefully with their hands in view. The pair rode directly toward the cattle camp. After a few

134

minutes they could easily be recognized as Big Ed MacWilliams and Sheriff Dan Sims.

"Wonder what brings them two away from the comforts of Duncan," Chaw remarked.

"Big Ed prob'ly misses our business," Doak Timmons said. "We ain't exactly been bellying up to that Deep River Saloon bar like we did in the past."

"He'd better not have brung no liquor out here with him," Doak Timmons said. "I got a no-drinking rule out here on the drive."

"There ain't nothing wrong with a nip, is there?" Chaw asked licking his lips. "It helps to cut the dust in a feller's throat."

"The rule is no drinking out here," Tim Hawkins said. "And that goes special for you boys from my Circle H Bar."

A couple of cowboys from the other outfits laughed out loud. It was common knowledge that the young man spent most evenings in Big Ed's place while his drovers stuck to their jobs out at the arroyo.

When Sheriff Sims spotted the body, he kicked his horse's flanks and cantered up to it. Dismounting, he knelt down and looked the man over. "Who done it?"

"A little bird," Chaw said. "A little bird with a big shooting iron."

Sims gave the old man a cold stare. "When I ask a question, I expect to be treated with respect like a law officer should be."

"I packed a star or two in my day," Chaw said. "And I'd never be pushy enough—or dumb enough—to ask much about a shot feller in a crowd o' cowboys out on the prairie."

"Well, you ain't me, are you?" Sims said. "Who shot this man?"

"I did," Rawley said. "Self-defense." He indicated

135

his bandaged shoulder and the sling.

Sims shrugged. "I reckon I got to take your word on that, Pierson."

"I reckon you do," Rawley said.

"Does anybody know him?" Sims asked.

"Sure," Rawley said. "His name's Walt Deacon. I had some run-ins with him before. Fact o' the matter, I was the one who brung him in on a charge that got him five years in the state prison."

"So he come out here for a showdown, huh?" the sheriff said. "Are you sure it wasn't the other way around?"

"What do you mean?" Rawley asked coldly.

"Maybe it was you that got a shaved head and striped suit," Sims said.

"You ain't calling me a liar, are you, Sheriff?"

Sims said nothing for a moment. He stared straight into Rawley's eyes before saying, "No, I ain't."

"He shot me from a distance with his Henry rifle," Rawley said.

"From a distance?" Sims asked. He looked again at the body. "He looks like he was hit close-up. His clothes is all powder-burnt. How'd that come about?"

"Like Chaw said—don't be pushy or dumb," Rawley said. "I say it's self-defense and that's what it is."

"Did he beat the shit out of you too?" Sims asked, looking at Rawley's face.

"Nope."

Sims, an observant man, had already seen how Tim Hawkins looked. "I reckon it was just a cowboy argument, huh?"

"I reckon," Rawley said.

Big Ed MacWilliams now noticed Tim's battered and swollen features. Surprised, he smiled and motioned to the young man to follow him away from the crowd a bit. When they were out of hearing, he said, "Looks like you and Pierson had a disagreement."

"We did," Tim said sullenly. "I got mad about him over Nancy."

Big Ed's expression darkened. "Has Pierson been bothering her?"

"No," Tim said, shaking his head. "They're declaring."

"What?" Big Ed clenched his teeth in a rage that he could barely keep a clamp on.

"That sonofabitch is prob'ly gonna be my brother-in-law," Tim said. "Nancy told me so herself. I come out here and jumped him about it."

Big Ed calmed down some. "Now, now, Tim. Don't you worry none. Ain't you and me been friends for a long time now? I'll help you outta this one."

"I'd be obliged, Big Ed," Tim said. "I don't like him one damn bit. And I particular don't want my sister marrying up with one o' the hands."

"I'll give you some help, just like I do with money," Big Ed said in a kindly tone.

"I'm obliged, Big Ed," Tim said gratefully.

The two walked back to the crowd. The Lazy S's Slim Watkins looked at Big Ed. "What brings you and the sheriff all the way out here? I know you didn't hear about this shooting."

Big Ed shrugged. "We don't see you fellers much and I didn't have nothing to do. Me and Dan was just flapping our jaws, so we decided to ride out and find out what's been going on."

"We been shooting no-good bushwhacking sonofabitches," Chaw Stevens said.

"That's easy to see," Big Ed remarked.

"Can you fellers spare us a cup of hot, strong coffee?" Sims asked.

"There's some over to the chuck wagon," Slim said. "Help yourself."

"By the way," the sheriff remarked. "Are you gonna bury Deacon or just let him rot?"

"We're gonna let the buzzards and coyotes have him," Chaw said.

"No. We'll stick him in the ground," Rawley said. "Not so much for respect as for keeping him from stinking up the range out here."

"It don't matter one way or the other to me," Sims said. "We got no undertaker in town anyhow." He tapped Big Ed's shoulder. "Let's get some o' that brew."

Both Big Ed and Sheriff Dan Sims enjoyed a leisurely cup of coffee. They chatted a bit with the ranchers while the cowboys went back to watching the cattle and guarding the camp. After an hour, the two remounted and rode back across the prairie toward town.

As soon as they were out of sight of the drovers, Sims chuckled and glanced over at Big Ed. "Well, so much for hiring Walt Deacon. I think that's what the feller meant when he talked about throwing good money after bad."

"That ain't funny," Big Ed snapped.

"I've heard of Rawley Pierson before," Sims said. "Him and that bow-legged sidekick kept things under control in a coupla towns that had got wild and woolly."

"If you know so much about 'em, how come you never mentioned that before?" Big Ed asked.

"Hell! It seemed to me that you could figger that out yourself after they kicked hell out of a coupla your boys. Or at least you should have had an inkling they was good in about any kind o' fight that come their way."

138

Big Ed clammed up. He rode the rest of the way into town seething inside. Hearing of Nancy Hawkins and Rawley Pierson had increased his hatred to an extent that he could barely think of the romance without trembling with rage.

When they reached the Deep River Saloon they found Calvin Witherspoon pacing back and forth on the porch. He watched them intently as they left their horses tied to the hitching rail and joined him.

"Well?" Witherspoon asked.

"Your boy got his ass shot," Sheriff Sims said. "He's dead as dead can be. The feller he tried to dry-gulch turned the game around on him."

"It seems our sheriff here knew more about Rawley Pierson than he told us," Big Ed said. "He's a hell of a hard man to take."

"Goddamn it!" Witherspoon cursed. "Deacon was supposed to shoot him from a distance!"

"He did," Big Ed said. "I don't know exactly what happened, but he hit Rawley in the shoulder from long range and Rawley shot him almost point-blank."

"That's impossible!" Witherspoon snapped.

Sims shrugged. "I kinda figger that when Pierson was hit, he went down into deep grass and prob'ly laid waiting for whoever shot him to show up."

"That makes sense," Big Ed said. "So when that dumb bastard walks to where he thinks he is, Pierson hauls off and puts a coupla slugs in him."

Witherspoon shook his head. "There is no reason why we shouldn't be in complete control of this situation. Yet things are happening that keep putting us behind schedule."

"Cattlemen ain't predictable when they're riled," Sims observed. "You ain't buying railroad stock here, Witherspoon. You're trying to run a bunch of tough

139

sonofabitches off'n their ranches!"

"We got to get Pierson," Big Ed insisted. "With him gone, we can handle the rest."

"What the hell do you want to do?" Witherspoon asked. "Spend a small fortune sending hired guns after him until one finally gets lucky to put in a killing shot?"

"Maybe we ought to use our brains and put some thoughts to this," Big Ed said.

Witherspoon barked a sarcastic laugh. "Now that'd be a big change, wouldn't it?"

"I don't see how there's much of a choice," Sims said. "That gang that was kept on a payroll has melted away mostly. Right now, we couldn't get a good raid on the cattle camp going if we wanted to."

"Now isn't this just great?" Witherspoon said aloud. He paced back and forth on the porch waving his arms up and down. "One cowboy and his broken-down pal have brought a million-dollar operation to a complete standstill."

"Calm down," Big Ed said. "And I wasn't joshing when I said it was time we tried something a hell of a lot smarter."

Sims looked over at the saloon owner. "You're beginning to sound like you might have something in mind, Big Ed."

Witherspoon suddenly felt hopeful. "Yeah. Has an idea sprung into your mind?"

"Not a complete one yet," Big Ed said. "But there's one way to get both Pierson and Chaw Stevens into a spot bad for 'em. We got a real ace in the hole for that."

"What are you talking about?" Witherspoon demanded.

Big Ed smiled. "Tim Hawkins."

"Anything in particular on your mind?" Sims asked.

"Well, first thing we got to do is throw some more

140

hot lead Pierson's way," Big Ed said. "I want him nervous and mean as hell."

"That means more money!" Witherspoon complained.

"Look at it this way," Big Ed said in a soothing tone. "If one of 'em happens to get lucky, we'll finally be ahead o' that damn schedule you keep talking about."

Chapter 15

The sky was overcast, making the weather a lot cooler than it had been for more than a week. The clouds, though high, did much to keep the sun off the Diablos. But Rawley Pierson wasn't enjoying the improvement much. Between boredom and his aching shoulder, he felt restless.

Shifting his arm in the sling from time to time, Rawley rode slowly along the arroyo rim keeping an eye on the milling cattle. He felt absolutely useless. There were enough men around to keep an eye out on things, and such pointless activity always made him edgy and nervous. As far as he was concerned, it was like the worst part of being a sheriff—the long tedious hours of waiting with nothing to do while the town was quiet and peaceful. Even if there was a raid on the camp, there was little he could do but fire at the attackers. He was in no shape to chase after the spoilers.

Finally, after his fifth circuit of the area, Rawley pulled on the reins of his horse and rode slowly outward toward the guards watching out on the Diablos for any unexpected visitors. He went past the limits of the camp and rode farther, moving slowly.

"Ho, Rawley!" Chaw Stevens's voice drifted across the prairie.

Rawley turned in his saddle and saw his friend a hundred yards away. He waved at him with his good arm. "Ho, Chaw!"

Chaw kicked his mount into a canter and crossed the flat terrain, drawing up close. "Where're you off to?"

"I just got tired o' riding around and around that damn arroyo," Rawley said. "There's five fellers and the cook there anyhow."

"That didn't answer my question," Chaw said. "Where're you off to?"

"I'm going over to where I gunned Walt Deacon," Rawley said. "There might be something there worth finding."

Chaw looked at the sling. "It don't appear like Deacon was onliest one that got gunned."

Rawley grinned weakly. "I reckon not. But I'll allow that between him and me, I'm the onliest one that can ride over there."

"And I'll allow how you're right. And speaking of getting shot, how's the shoulder?" Chaw inquired.

"Kinda paining me, but it makes me feel more mad than hurt," Rawley answered.

"You'd best be careful," Chaw warned him. "If that thing gets all pusy and puffed up, you're gonna be in a lotta trouble. There ain't no doctor in Duncan, y'know." He eyed Rawley suspiciously. "Are you planning on doing something real dumb?"

"Nope."

"You do a lotta dumb things, Rawley," Chaw reminded him. "Like when you went into the saloon in Benton after them three Mexicans without waiting for me."

Rawley nodded. "That was dumb," he agreed.

"And then there was the time you went out to the

143

Claxton ranch to serve them papers," Chaw said. "That was dumb."

"That was dumb," Rawley repeated.

"And then—"

"Do I gotta hear ever' dumb thing I did in my whole life?" Rawley asked.

"The Good Lord ain't give this earth enough time for that," Chaw said. "Anyhow, what're you gonna do over there where you shot ol' Deacon?"

"I already told you. I'm just gonna look around," Rawley said.

"For what?"

"For whatever I can find, goddamn it!" Rawley snapped.

"I'll go with you," Chaw said, ignoring his friend's testiness.

"You'll get your damn butt bit bad by the boss if you leave here," Rawley said. "He really don't give a hoot what I do on account o' my wing got bent."

Chaw was thoughtful for a few moments. "I reckon you're right."

"See you later."

"See you later. And don't do nothing dumb." Chaw turned and rode back to his position on the perimeter of the cattle camp.

Rawley pulled on the reins and his horse took the hint, clomping out farther onto the Diablos. Man and animal traveled slowly for more than an hour. Although it remained overcast and cloudy, the afternoon gave no hint of rain. From time to time Rawley peered toward the horizon to see if distant showers could be seen streaming out of the clouds, and he sniffed to see if any dampness rode the wind. But it was only a cloud cover, promising no moisture for the great plains country.

Finally he reached the place where he and Walt

Deacon had each made the choice to fight to the death. The mashed buffalo grass hadn't recovered much. A rust-colored expanse on the thick growth showed where Deacon gave up the ghost. The wounds in his skull and chest had been massive.

Rawley carefully held his slung arm outward as he slowly swung out of the saddle. He walked around studiously, then noticed some gray gook on the ground. Rawley squatted down to look at it, then quickly stood up when he realized it was pieces of Deacon's brain.

Carefully remounting, he traced the crushed grass back to Deacon's ambush site. When he reached it, he looked over to where he'd been shot. No doubt about it, Deacon had done some fancy shooting. If the strike of the bullet had been two inches to the left, it would have hit Rawley just to the side of the base of his neck. If that hadn't killed him, then he'd have lain there while Deacon came over and finished him off at his leisure.

Rawley studied the ground some more, and could see where Deacon had ridden in from to reach the site. He rode around for a half hour in what seemed aimless circles until he realized that was the exact path Deacon had taken when tracking him and moving into a position within killing range.

"The son of a bitch!" Rawley said to himself.

He was thoughtful for several moments, then decided to see how far he could backtrack the bushwhacker. This was a luxury that none of the ranchers had been able to enjoy in the past. If Rawley was lucky he might find where the raiders' former camp was. If he was even luckier, he'd find it was still occupied. But if all his luck was bad, the raiders would discover him too—and a lone man stood no chance against an entire gang. Especially one with a shot-up shoulder who couldn't fire back or ride well.

145

Once again Rawley dismounted. This time, leading his horse by the reins, he walked slowly along as he traced Deacon's trail through the high, thick grass of the Diablos Range. It was slow going when the ground began to dip where some ancient river had once flowed across the land in days before even the Indians had come there. Deacon, wanting to keep out of sight as much as possible, had chosen the route for the cover it afforded.

Rawley's shoulder began throbbing a bit as the extra physical effort of negotiating the rough terrain caused him to stumble a few times. He came out of the dry riverbed after a half hour and traced Deacon's route up onto the flatlands. Rawley stood there, breathing a bit heavily after the effort, and surveyed the Diablos.

The range had a stark beauty. The vast emptiness and levelness were breathtaking with a sameness that depicted repetitive grandeur rather than monotony. Rawley felt dwarfed by the magnitude of that great land. He knew that the day was fast approaching when sodbusters and their wives would show up with wagon loads of kids, belongings, and barbed wire to fence off the unrestrained beauty and ruin it for cattlemen forever. At that moment, he hated them for it.

And he then truly knew how the Indians must have felt when the first ranchers moved onto the great central plains.

Rawley got back to the job at hand, once again following the matted trail through the grass. Another half hour went by, and he came to an abrupt halt. The trail led to a spot where two other horses had shown up. By walking around the area, Rawley deduced that Deacon had met somebody there. Remnants of a cook fire were off to one side. Deacon had scraped away the grass down to bare ground in order to build it there. That meant he'd probably spent the night waiting for whoever it was that had shown up.

He found where Deacon had slept. It was a ways from where the fire had been. If someone had been attracted to the area by the light thrown off by dying embers, they would not have found the camper easily. Rawley nodded approvingly. That was a good way to avoid any nasty surprises in the middle of the night.

A few more moments of looking around and Rawley deduced that the visitors had come from the north— the direction of the town of Duncan where Big Ed MacWilliams kept his Deep River Saloon. Rawley nodded. Whoever those people were, they were undoubtedly the ones who'd given Deacon the hundred dollars to put a slug in him.

Rawley decided to ignore whoever had come from town. Instead, he searched the ground some more until he was able to find where Walt Deacon had come in from. The trail led off toward the west. Rawley put his foot in his stirrup and swung up over the saddle. The sudden effort sent a wave of dizziness sweeping through him with such force that his vision blurred. The shoulder flared up, and for a moment he thought he was going to vomit.

Taking deep, even breaths brought him back to normal. Cursing Deacon and his rifle, Rawley urged his horse on as he began following the track that led out across the sweeping panorama of the Diablos Range.

By then the clouds had begun to break up, letting the hot rays of the sun shine through the thinning layer. The weather gradually warmed, growing hotter as the brightness increased. Dryness attacked Rawley's throat with an intensity he hadn't known since he'd ridden across the arid Staked Plains of New Mexico. He took frequent drinks from his canteen, but it didn't seem to help much.

Rawley licked his lips and reached up to rub his hand

147

across his brow. As hot as he was, he should have been sweating profusely, but his skin was hot and dry. Now concerned, and pretty sure about what was happening, Rawley touched his wounded shoulder. It was so warm it seemed a fire burned there. At that moment he knew the worst. The injury had gotten infected. There was nothing to do but return to camp and turn himself over to Chaw's less-than-tender medical care. But what the old man lacked in gentleness, he made up with real practical knowledge in the treatment of all sorts of hurts and sickness.

Rawley had pulled on the reins to change the direction of travel when the voice off to the side startled him.

"Hold it, mister!"

Rawley snapped his eyes to his right and saw an armed man with a bandanna across the bottom of his face. There was only one reason why he would be out that far on the Diablos. He was one of the raiders. Undoubtedly a lookout, he probably didn't have his hood with him, so he'd used his kerchief to hide his face. Rawley decided to play dumb. "Hell! I ain't got no money."

"I seen you before," the man said, keeping his carbine barrel trained straight on Rawley. "You're that feller from the cattle camp."

Rawley, the increasing fever burning in his brain, had to think fast. Grimacing with pain, he edged his arm out of the sling so he could get his hand down to the backup derringer in his belt. "I ain't from no cattle camp," Rawley said. "I'm crossing this range on my way to—" He pulled the derringer and fired the first barrel. He missed.

The gunman, startled and angered, blasted a shot at Rawley that zipped harmlessly past his face. He worked the cocking lever to chamber another of the big

.44-caliber bullets.

Rawley cut loose with the second barrel of the small pistol. The slug slammed into the man's chest, turning him slightly. He dropped the carbine and sank to his knees. Shouting in the near distance caught Rawley's attention. He saw a half-dozen men riding toward him. Digging the spurs into his horse, Rawley bolted for safety. His horse collided with the kneeling man, bowling him over as Rawley began a run across the range.

Now Rawley was in one hell of a bad way. His infected shoulder burst into agonizing spasms of pain as the arm bounced loosely at his side. Nausea and dizziness swept over him, making breathing difficult as he fought the urge to vomit. Gritting his teeth, Rawley held onto the reins with his good hand and concentrated on keeping his seat in the saddle during the wild ride.

Bullets split the air around him as Rawley continued his galloping escape. The pounding of hooves and jerking around in the saddle caused his fever-induced confusion to increase until for moments at a time he actually was unaware of what he was doing. Rawley's vision clouded over and he could no longer focus his eyes. The world around him turned into a blurry mass and his breath came in hot gasps. But deep inside his brain, the strong will to survive kept a spark alive that helped him stick to the back of the horse even when the ride carried him and his pursuers onto a rolling, dipping portion of the Diablos.

His mind was barely aware when the sound of shooting increased and the shadowy figures of riders seemed to be flitting all around him. Once again he fought the waves of nausea and fainting as best he could, but finally it was all too much.

Rawley didn't feel the ground when he hit it, nor was

he aware of bouncing and rolling. He lay on his back, blinking his eyes, trying to bring himself back into some sense of balance or awareness. A blurry face appeared above his, and Rawley tried to speak. But all he could do was gasp.

"Well," said Chaw's welcome voice. "Looks like you just did one more dumb thing."

Chapter 16

Rawley opened his eyes. Although he had a slight headache, he was strangely comfortable and cool. He was in the shade, without the hot sun glaring down on him to increase the fever that racked his brain. Then he realized there was no burning in his head and he was also no longer outdoors. Rawley could see a white ceiling above him.

The injured man tried to sit up, but a wave of dizziness forced him down. But the effort showed him that he was lying in a nice bed between clean sheets. A door opened, and he turned his face toward the sound.

"You're awake!" Nancy Hawkins exclaimed.

Rawley said nothing, only staring incredulously at this most welcome sight of the woman he loved.

"Can't you speak?" she asked with a concerned expression on her face.

"Yeah," Rawley said. His voice was strangely weak, no more than a hoarse whisper. He cleared his throat and tried again. "Yeah." That sounded better. "I'm awake, but I sure don't know what's going on."

Nancy had a pitcher of water and a towel with her. She walked over to him and kissed him lightly on the forehead before turning to the nightstand and filling a glass that sat there.

"That looks mighty inviting," Rawley said.

"Let me help you," Nancy offered.

Rawley struggled as she aided him in sitting up enough to take a drink. The water was delicious in his dry mouth and he swallowed eagerly.

"That's enough for now," Nancy said. She gently lowered him back down. She dampened the cloth and laid it across Rawley's forehead. "Now you should feel a little better."

"I feel a whole lot better," Rawley said. He frowned in puzzlement. "How did I get here? I'm in the ranch house, ain't I?"

"Yes," Nancy answered. "Chaw and the boys brought you in."

"When was this?" Rawley asked.

"Two days ago," Nancy answered. "Now you relax and I'll tell you what happened."

Rawley listened as the young woman related what she'd heard from the Circle H Bar cowboys when they'd brought him in. He'd been chased quite a ways by some of the masked outlaws, and had just managed to stay ahead of them when the rest of the drovers arrived on the scene after hearing all the shooting.

"I think I remember a sorta shootout with a feller," Rawley said.

"When they found you, you'd fallen from your horse," Nancy explained. "Chaw checked you over and found your shoulder wound had gotten infected. It was so bad, he insisted that you be brought in."

Rawley smiled weakly. "I reckon he had to argue with Tim about that, right?"

"I'm afraid so," Nancy said. She sat down carefully on the edge of the bed to keep from shaking him too much. "Frankly, Chaw didn't know if you would make it or not. And to complicate things, Tim wanted to put you in the bunkhouse, but I had them bring you here into Papa's room."

Rawley looked at his shoulder. "It don't feel too bad now. Ol' Chaw musta done a good job o' cleaning it out."

"I took care of it," Nancy said. "I used carbolic acid."

"What in the world is that?"

"A doctor passing through left some," Nancy said. "It's good to keep wounds from festering. He let us have a few other things we'd need since there's no doctor anywhere on the Diablos or in Duncan. He explained that carbolic acid is supposed to be used to clean a hurt when it's fresh, but it gets rid of infection too sometimes after a wound hasn't been tended to for a while."

"Well," Rawley said. "I got to admit my shoulder feels better'n it did a coupla days ago."

"You had a lot of fever, but it broke last night," Nancy said.

"Last night? Was you with me all night?"

"Last night, yesterday, the night before, and most of the first day," Nancy said. "That's when they brought you in." She leaned over and kissed him again. "I was pretty worried."

"You were, huh?"

"At least until the fever broke," Nancy said. "Then I knew for sure you'd be all right."

"It looks like we're gonna spend some time together we didn't know we'd have," Rawley said.

"That's the blessing part of you getting hurt," Nancy said. "You won't be getting out of bed for at least three or four more days."

"I'm gonna have to get back to the cattle camp," Rawley insisted.

"Sure," Nancy said. "Do you want me to go out and saddle your horse for you right now?"

153

The words emphasized his physical weakness to him as he lay in the bed. Rawley slowly shook his head and grinned. "I reckon not. I don't think I could pull myself out of this bed right now."

She gave him another drink. "You'll be needing the night pot now that you're going to be drinking water."

Rawley's face reddened a bit at the thought of urinating into the container under the bed. But he knew he'd have to sooner or later and it would be up to Nancy to empty it for him.

"Oh, don't be so embarrassed!" she said. "I've got a father and a brother, and I've had to look after them when they were ailing from time to time. We'll be married soon anyway. So there won't be any secrets of that sort between us."

"By the time I need the outhouse, I'll be able to walk, believe me!" Rawley exclaimed.

"You'll have to eat first," Nancy said. "Do you feel hungry at all?"

"I can't say that I do," Rawley answered. "Is that a bad sign?"

"There's nothing to worry about. It'll take a day or so for you to get your appetite back," Nancy said. "You're so dried out from fever that it'll be water that you need first."

Rawley started to speak again, but a wave of fatigue swept over him with such suddenness it almost frightened him. "Dang me! I don't know what happened. But in just the flicker of an eye I've got so— so tired."

Nancy gently laid her hand on his brow. "Sleep then, dear. That's what you need more than anything. Lots of rest to build up your strength."

Rawley fought to stay awake, but his eyes closed as if by their own independent will, and he drifted off into a deep, dreamless, and restful slumber.

When he awoke later it was dark outside. Rawley turned his head slightly, and could see the dancing light of a lantern out in the hall that led to the kitchen. He licked his dry lips, and was about to call out for a drink of water when he head Tim's voice in the other room.

"How long is he gonna be laid up there?"

"As long as it takes him to get well!" Nancy snapped back at her brother.

"The cattle drive is only a couple of weeks away," Tim said.

"He'll be ready by then," Nancy said. "Don't worry."

"He better be," Tim said sullenly. "I'll see you later."

"I see you've taken a bath and changed clothes. I suppose that means you're heading into town," Nancy said.

"Yeah," Tim said. "But not before I say a nice howdy to good ol' Rawley Pierson."

"He's sleeping," Nancy said.

"If he is, I won't wake him up," Tim growled. "I just want to see how he looks."

"Not out of concern, I imagine," Nancy said.

"Not much," Tim replied.

Rawley could hear the heavy tread of Tim's boots as he walked toward the bedroom. The door opened and Tim stepped inside. "Well, Pierson. Looks like you're awake."

"Are my eyes open?" Rawley asked.

"Yeah."

"Then I'm awake," he said.

"That's pretty damn funny," Tim said sarcastically. "Are you planning on staying in that bed for the rest o' your life, or are you gonna be giving me and the boys a hand? We still got raiders to deal with and a cattle drive to make."

"I'll be up before long," Rawley said. "You can stop my pay while I'm laid up if you want."

"I oughta," Tim said. "But I wouldn't want you to think I was being mean to you." He turned and walked back to the living room where Nancy was. "Looks like he's gonna live."

"I hope that doesn't bother you, Tim," Nancy said coldly.

"I'm always a happy man," Tim replied. "Well, I'm leaving now. I'll be back before morning."

"Suit yourself," Nancy remarked.

Tim hurried out of the house and mounted his horse. After a glance at the window of the bedroom where Rawley lay recuperating, Tim rode out to the road and turned toward Duncan.

He rode easily for an hour, a feeling of apprehension building up in him as it always did lately. Before, when he'd been a surefire winner at poker, he'd gone into Duncan feeling so happy he was almost giddy. But his self-confidence had been badly rattled by his losses at the gaming table and the growing debt to Big Ed MacWilliams.

Tim rode into town, passing Mrs. Malone's boardinghouse. He went straight up to the front of the Deep River Saloon. Big Ed and his friend Calvin Witherspoon sat in chairs on the porch. Shorty Clemens stood beside them, leaning up against one of the posts that supported the roof overhead.

Tim dismounted and walked up to them. "Howdy. It looks like you boys are enjoying the season's nice weather."

"Yeah. The spring is always nice after a long winter. And how're you doing, Tim?" Big Ed asked with a wide smile. "And how's Pierson doing?"

"I reckon he'll make it," Tim said.

Shorty spat a stream of tobacco juice. "I thought them raiders had done you a favor on him."

"He's a tough sonofabitch," Tim said. He nodded to

156

Cal Witherspoon. "Howdy, Mister Witherspoon."

"Hello, Tim. Are you going to try your luck at cards again?" he asked. "You came mighty close the other night."

"I'm getting luckier," Tim said. "I can feel it in my bones." He tried to put a cheerful tone in his voice. "Are you playing tonight, Shorty?"

"Sure! Let's get going," Shorty said. He walked toward the door.

Tim followed as Big Ed got out of his chair and accompanied him into the saloon. They went through their usual procedure of going to the office. But Big Ed had no money to give Tim from the safe. Instead he passed a hundred dollars to him that he pulled out of his own pocket.

"How much does this make, Big Ed?" Tim asked.

Big Ed smiled. "Don't worry about it, Tim. We'll square it all in the end."

"I really appreciate this," Tim said. "And you'll get ever' cent back, believe me."

"I believe you, Tim," Big Ed said with a smile.

Tim went back out to the table, where a game was already in progress. After the hand being played was settled up, he grabbed a chair. "What's the ante, boys?"

"Five dollars," Curly Brandon said. It was Curly's turn to deal. "And the name o' the game is draw poker. Open on jacks or better."

Tim sat sullenly as his five cards slid across the table from him. When he had them all, he picked them up. He had a pair of kings, an ace, an eight, and a three. Nobody else could open and he started out cautiously. "Five dollars, boys."

Hank DeLong eyed him carefully. "Sure, Tim. Let's just play along with that."

There were no raises and Tim turned in the eight and three. He got back another pair of kings for his trouble.

Trying to look nonchalant, he bet cautiously. "How's about keeping that to five dollars?"

Hank raised it another five, then Joe Black did the same. When the cards were laid down, Tim raked in a pot of eighty dollars.

Tim grinned slightly. "Well! That ain't a bad start, is it?"

"Damn, Tim!" Shorty said. "You ain't going back to your old ways, are you?"

Rosalie and Hannah walked up to the table to watch as the pasteboards began to be played seriously. Big Ed produced a bottle, and the drinks were taken steadily as the evening's poker activity rolled on.

And Tim Hawkins could do nothing wrong.

His winnings had gone up to over five hundred before Shorty Clemens finally stood up. "I'm going out for some fresh air before that damn Tim wins all that too."

Tim, half drunk, laughed. "You better watch out, all right! Me and these here playing cards is singing pretty together tonight. Yes, sir!"

Shorty passed Big Ed coming in to see how the game was going. The saloon owner winked at his hired gun. "How's it panning out, Shorty?"

Shorty grinned. "We're giving him a taste o' the good ol' days, Big Ed. He's lapping it up like a thirsty cow at a rangeland creek." He walked outside to the porch and pulled a cigar from his leather vest.

Calvin Witherspoon glanced at him. "It sounds like young Tim Hawkins is having quite a night."

"Just like we planned," Shorty said, lighting his cigar.

Witherspoon got up and went over to the batwing doors and peered inside. "I see Big Ed is keeping an eye on things."

158

"He's just making sure none o' the boys pull in anything for themselves," Shorty said.

Witherspoon turned and walked over to him. "I know a way you could get an extra couple of hundred."

Shorty looked at him. "How's that, Mister Witherspoon."

"I want you to have about three of those rascals camping out there on the range to go to the Circle H Bar and finish off Pierson," Witherspoon said.

Shorty shook his head. "Big Ed won't put up with that. There's too much danger to the Hawkins girl. If something was to happen to her, the feller that done it could be sure of getting stomped to death."

"If Big Ed isn't careful, he's going to find himself on the outside looking in," Witherspoon said. "The only way this deal is going to be wrapped up—and the big payoffs made—is to ruin those ranchers. If the drive to Kansas is made, you can forget about any success for at least a year. And with Pierson around, that might not be possible. Get my drift?"

"Sure, Mister Witherspoon," Shorty said. "But I'd hate like hell to get Big Ed riled at me."

"I'll give you one hundred dollars to set up a raid on that ranch and a hundred each to the gunmen who do the actual shooting," Witherspoon said. "Do you think that makes it worthwhile?"

"Yes, sir," Shorty said. "But if there's gunplay around the house, Nancy Hawkins might accidental get shot like I said."

"Do you really give a damn, Shorty?"

Shorty grinned. "No, sir. But Big Ed is gonna give one great big damn. Count on it."

"I'll take care of Big Ed, don't worry about that," Witherspoon assured him. "The question at this point is: Do you want that money?"

"I sure do, Mister Witherspoon. It'll take a coupla days to set things up."

"Then get to it," Witherspoon said.

Shorty nodded. "I'll get started first thing in the morning, Mister Witherspoon."

"Don't forget," Witherspoon said.

"For a hunnerd dollars? It ain't likely!"

Chapter 17

Rawley walked unsteadily, his arm around Nancy's shoulders while she held onto his waist as they made their way slowly from the parlor back toward the bedroom.

"Don't try to rush," Nancy said. "Let's take our time."

The big man fought the waves of dizziness that swept over him. The sensation was so strong that it made his vision blur.

"Keep going, darling," Nancy urged him. "Just a few more steps and we'll be back to the bed."

He took a deep breath and finally made it to their destination, sitting down for a moment before lying back. "Now that was a job, wasn't it?"

"It's your first time out of bed, darling," Nancy said covering him up. "That walk to the parlor and back was just what you needed." She adjusted his pillow, then sat down on the edge of the bed. "An infection like you had saps the strength something awful."

"I sure thought I'd be a lot more stronger'n that," Rawley said in a discouraged tone. "I been eating right good. I figgered that was enough to bring me out of it."

"Your appetite is fine and that's a good sign," Nancy

161

said. "But you still have a ways to go."

"I come out of it a coupla days ago," he said. Rawley struggled to sit up, but couldn't quite make it. "Aw!" he exclaimed in disappointment. "Damn! By all rights I should be doing a lot better by now."

"Not necessarily. And don't you try to push it," Nancy cautioned him. "How about some more soup?"

He nodded. "If that's what it's gonna take to get the fire back in me, then bring it on." He frowned. "Has Tim been around looking for me to get back to work?"

"Don't you give that brother of mine another thought," Nancy told him. "He came back from that last trip into town a couple of nights ago and went straight out to the cattle camp the next morning. With you gone, he's probably got to do some work for a change."

"He never seemed to like it out there too much," Rawley said.

"I'm glad he's got to stick to his job," Nancy said. "That card-playing of his causes me too much worry."

"He ain't been betting any ranch belongings or land, has he?" Rawley asked.

"I don't think so," Nancy said. "But as the male heir he can do anything with the property he wants, and there's no way I can stop any foolishness."

"I'm sure Tim ain't gonna do nothing that stupid," Rawley said.

"We'd better stop talking and let you rest," Nancy said standing up. "I'll go get you that bowl of soup."

"That's what I need," Rawley said. He closed his eyes as she left the room. The walk around the house had worn him out more than he would admit. Between dizziness and weak legs, he hadn't been sure he was even going to make it.

A few minutes later Nancy was back with a bowl of hot chicken soup. She'd put in some wild onions and summer peas to flavor it up. "Can you sit up now?"

"Lemme try," Rawley said. It took him a few minutes, but he managed to get up to a sitting position. He leaned back against the headboard. "Ain't I strong? I sat up all by myself."

"You're a good boy," Nancy said, smiling. She spooned up some of the soup and fed him. "How's that?"

"Delicious," Rawley said sincerely. He took a couple of more mouthfuls, then leaned back to rest a bit. "The way I figger things, we can get hitched right after the drive to Kansas, right?"

"If that's what you want," Nancy said.

"O'course I do," Rawley said. "And if the Good Lord's willing and the creeks don't rise, I'll have my pay for us to start out on. The only thing is deciding just what place we're gonna go to."

Nancy looked around the room. "I hate to leave this house. I was born in it and lived here all my life." She fed him some more soup.

"Well, darling, I reckon we can't stay here," Rawley said. "Tim wouldn't put up with that."

"I'm ashamed he's my brother sometimes," Nancy said bitterly.

"He'll grow up later on, dear," Rawley assured her. "It'll all work out in the end. You wait and see. Him and us will end up visiting a lot with each other. And I bet it won't take too long neither."

"I hope you're right," Nancy said.

"Sure I am."

"I was kind of hoping that we could stay on here and you could be the foreman," Nancy said.

"I think we better think on starting our own spread," Rawley said.

"That will be difficult on the Diablos," Nancy said. "There's about as many ranches now as this area

163

can support."

"There's always the Cherokee Strip," Rawley suggested. "A feller can get a good deal on land from the Indians up there. I'll have enough money to get a few head o' cattle."

"Perhaps Chaw will go in with us on the venture," Nancy said.

"You wouldn't mind that?" Rawley asked hopefully.

"Of course not!" Nancy chided. "I think old Chaw is a perfectly delightful man."

"I'll ask him," Rawley said. "I reckon he'll go along with us. With him chipping in on it, we'll have a bigger herd. He and I can do some looking in on this while we're up there in Dodge city. There's fellers in that town that know all about what's going on in the cattle business in any part o' the country you care to look into."

"Here. Take some more soup," Nancy said.

The meal, small as it was, made Rawley feel better. A pleasant warmth spread through him, and the trembling weakness that had plagued him moments before eased up a bit.

"How's that shoulder?" Nancy asked.

"A little sore," Rawley said.

"That means it must hurt a lot," Nancy scolded. "You always cover up when you're in pain."

"Well, I could sure complain about the way it itches, if you want to know the truth," Rawley admitted.

"That's a good sign," Nancy advised him. "It means it's clean and healing nicely."

"Can I scratch it?"

"No!" She kept feeding him for another ten minutes until the bowl was finished. "Want some more, darling?"

Rawley shook his head. "I reckon as to how I'm full. Maybe later."

Nancy glanced outside at the growing dusk. "It'll be dark soon. You probably should go to sleep."

He settled down on the bed as she fixed up the pillow again. "A good night's sleep sounds like heaven itself," he said. "I'll be stronger in the morning and really walk around this old house."

"We'll see," Nancy said, arranging the quilt.

"Why, in another coupla days I'll run all the way down to Mexico just to fetch us some chili peppers," Rawley said.

Nancy laughed. She bent down and kissed him on the mouth. "Go to sleep, darling."

Rawley smiled as his eyes slowly closed. He listened to the sounds of Nancy's soft footsteps as she left the bedroom and walked across the parlor. The extreme fatigue made slumber sweep over him fast and deep. Within moments he was lost to the world, his breath even and deep as he slept.

Rawley didn't dream. He had sunk into a heavy, natural unconsciousness that his body used as it continued going through the process of healing itself and recovering from the infection and trauma of being hit by a large-caliber rifle slug. He finally came awake some hours later when it was completely dark outside.

Rawley turned his head and glanced out the window, noting that the moon was behind clouds. At that moment he realized what had awakened him. He felt a stirring to relieve himself. Rawley fought it as long as he could, but finally had to answer nature's call. Slowly, laboriously he slid from under the covers until he was on his knees on the floor. Reaching under the bed he pulled out the chamber pot, breathing in relief as he urinated fully and forcibly. No doubt about it. The dehydration from the fever was gone. Letting go of that much water meant things were back to normal in that part of the process of getting better.

When he finished, he slid the pot back and leaned against the bed resting. Suddenly a sense of uneasiness flashed through him. There seemed to be no reason for the nervousness, but it was too strong to be denied.

Rawley held his breath as he listened, but could hear nothing. Reaching out to where his pistol sat on the lower shelf of the bedstand, he grasped it and brought it close to him. He slowly got to his feet. When he was fully erect, he felt another wave of dizziness, but he angrily fought it. This was no time to let a weakness take over.

Moving deliberately he went to the window and peered out into the ranch yard. It was dark and moonless, the features of objects barely visible in the deep gloom. But he could perceive no movement. Rawley still realized he was acting on naked instinct, that he couldn't be sure that he'd actually heard anything, but he'd damned well felt some sort of sensation that made him nervous. The cowboy realized it could be nothing but edginess due to his injury, but he didn't want to take any chances. He decided to walk around the house.

He'd just reached the bedroom door when the window behind him broke and a half-dozen rapid shots blasted in from outside. Rawley whirled and caught the glimpse of a man in the sudden, bright flashes of gunfire. He raised his pistol and squeezed the trigger. The recoil of the weapon tipped him off balance and, in his weakness, he staggered backward into the parlor to collide with the sofa before hitting the floor.

"Rawley!" Nancy's scream seemed to fill the house.

"I'm all right," he yelled back. "Stay put!"

"The hell if I will!" she retorted. Seconds later, her shadowy figure appeared at the foot of the stairs. "Where are you?"

"By the sofa," he answered in a whisper. "Keep your

voice down. I think there's several of 'em outside the house."

She joined him on the floor, cradling a Winchester carbine. "What happened?"

"Some sonofabitch tried to shoot me in bed, but I was at the door," Rawley said.

He noted the weapon she held. "Where in the world did you get that?"

"I always have one by my bed," she answered. "Anyhow, what were you doing here in the parlor? You know you're not supposed to walk around."

"Sweet love," Rawley pointed out, "if I hadn't been walking around, I'd be a bloody mess in there right now." He put his hand on her mouth. "Don't talk. We got to listen."

There were no sounds for a few moments, then some scuttling could be heard on three sides of the house. Finally there was some quick, whispered speaking before silence settled in again.

"There's more'n one of 'em out there, all right," Rawley said.

"We've got a fight on our hands," Nancy said. "I guess those raiders finally decided to hit a ranch instead of a cattle camp or isolated cowboys."

"I'd say you was right," Rawley agreed.

"How're you feeling, dear?"

"I was dizzy," Rawley said. "But right now I figger that's the least o' my problems."

Nancy started to speak, but she stopped. "Shhh!"

"The front door," Rawley whispered.

The portal rattled slightly. Like all the ranch houses, this one was never locked. The intruder slowly pushed it open and stepped inside.

Nancy raised the Winchester and fired. The bullet, flying at an upward angle, hit the man under the rib cage. He was flung back out the door to sprawl onto the

167

front porch.

More noise came from another part of the house. Nancy grasped Rawley's arm. "The kitchen! They're coming in through the kitchen!"

Rawley, on his hands and knees, turned in that direction. Once more the insidious dizziness hit him hard. He tried to ignore it, but he lost his balance and tumbled over on his side. Rawley could hear the sound of scuffling boots on the kitchen floor, moving fast toward the door that separated him and Nancy from the interlopers.

"I don't like uninvited people in my kitchen!" Nancy hissed under her breath. She raised up as the first man came into the parlor. The Winchester discharged, and the explosion was followed by a lightning-quick working of the cocking lever. The carbine blasted again.

"Oof!" A man spun around and staggered across the room toward the open front door. He almost made it before sprawling across the parlor floor.

Now Rawley was on his feet. He lurched unsteadily toward the door, damning the dizzy feeling and fighting it with every ounce of inner strength he possessed. He charged into the kitchen and saw a man's silhouette faintly framed in the window. He fired a snap shot.

A blast filled the room as did a quick flash of light. The doorjamb by Rawley's head exploded, hitting him with splinters. Desperately he emptied his revolver in the direction of the attack.

A thud on the floor was so heavy and sudden that it shook the house. Rawley instantly squatted down to make himself as small a target as possible. But no other shots followed. The only sound in the kitchen was shallow, labored breathing. Rawley knew he'd hit the raider bad.

"Darling?" Nancy's voice sounded from the parlor.

"I'm all right," Rawley said. "Be quiet. We got to listen."

Several long moments passed without a sound. Finally Rawley cautiously went to the window and peered out. Nothing seemed to move in the ranch yard. Exercising a great deal of caution, he went to the back door and stood quietly in apprehensive vigilance. After a few minutes he went back toward the parlor and called out to Nancy, "Bring a lantern."

Moments later, Nancy came in with the illumination. They walked over to the man in the kitchen. He was an enormous fellow, and a quick examination showed he'd be dead in moments. The thick scent of wood smoke hung over him, giving evidence he'd been out camping for some time. They went back to the parlor and found the man Nancy had shot in the house. He was a smaller man, but shared the same campfire odor with the other.

Next they went to the porch and checked the man out there. He too was dead, and also smelled of smoke.

"You done for him too," Rawley said. "There should be one more by the bedroom window."

They walked cautiously around the house and found the first man. Even Rawley winced at the sight in the lantern light. Most of his face had been blown off his skull. From the pistolero's nose down was nothing but a gaping, red wound.

Nancy was too concerned about Rawley to care much about the horrible spectacle lying at their feet. "Are you sure you're all right, darling?"

"I think that weakness kinda went away in the excitement," he said. "Maybe that's what I needed—a damn good scare."

"That's four of them gone," Nancy said in a weak voice. "I hope that's enough to finally put a stop to all this trouble."

Rawley shook his head. "I don't think so. But it's going to really bring this range war out into the open and it'll end up one way or the other pretty damn quick."

"One way or the other?" Nancy asked.

"I've seen these situations before, sweetheart," Rawley said. "And there's always a winner and a loser. No draws. And right now it's a toss-up as to how it'll end for us."

Chapter 18

Rawley, in old Zeb Hawkins's former bedroom, put the rest of his things in the saddlebags and carried them out to the kitchen. "Well," he said to Nancy. "I'm packed up and ready to settle into the bunkhouse."

"It doesn't take much for a cowboy to pack up and move, does it?" Nancy asked.

"It sure don't," Rawley agreed. "Or in my case, I reckon you could say the same thing about a feller that was a sheriff once. You don't collect much luxuries in that line o' work neither. Just about all a feller's belongings fit real well into a coupla saddlebags."

It had been three days since the raid on the ranch. Rawley's recovery had gone quickly after the excitement, and he felt almost as good as new.

The dead men were completey unknown to anyone on the Diablos. Their crime earned them unmarked graves out on the stark rangeland. After the four raiders had been buried, the Diablos Range Cattlemen's Association held a meeting. The animated conversation brought them around to a decision that at least one armed man would be kept at each ranch house from then on. Before the attack on the Circle H Bar, most of the ranchers figured that when the big showdown came between them and the raiders, it would be at the cattle camp.

As Slim Watkins of the Lazy S said during the debate, "We got 'em down to a number where they got to shit or get off the pot. They figger they can wreck the cattle drive by hitting the houses, so I reckon we'd better be ready to defend both our homes and the herd."

"I ain't leaving my missus and kids alone," Doak Timmons said. That put the idea of guarding the ranch houses into effect. "There's gonna be either me or one o' my boys handy at the Diamond T till this thing is over and did with."

"That's something we're all gonna be doing," said Ted Lawson of the Flying Heart as he echoed Slim's opinion.

Since it was still doubtful that Rawley could put in a full day's work at the herd, and since he'd need all his strength for the drive into Kansas, Tim reluctantly chose him to be the Circle H Ranch's home guard. Additionally, because Tim was worried about Nancy's safety, he wanted to make sure Rawley had a backup in case his physical strength slipped again. So the young ranch owner assigned Chaw Stevens to stay with Rawley in the bunkhouse. That meant that Jim Pauley and Duane Wheeler would stay with the herd. Tim planned on going back and forth between both places.

Chaw and Tim were due to ride into the ranch in the late afternoon. Rawley sat in the kitchen sipping coffee and watching Nancy cook as they waited for the pair to come in from the Diablos. Nancy pulled a pan of biscuits out of the wood-burning oven. She glanced up at her future husband. "It's only about another week and a half before the cattle drive."

"Yeah," Rawley said. "That's gonna be the big test too. Once we get that herd moving, them raiders is

172

gonna have to stop us there once and for all."

"Or *before* you start the drive," Nancy pointed out. She handed Rawley a large carving knife. "Make yourself useful and cut some slices off that ham."

"Yes, ma'am," Rawley said. He tended to the task, continuing to talk. "Like I told you the other night when them owlhoots tried to get us in the house. One way or the other, this range war is gonna come to an end. We'll have it all, or they'll have it all. There ain't gonna be no in-between."

"I'm afraid you're right about that," Nancy agreed. She glanced out the window. "Here comes Tim and Chaw."

The sound of hooves grew louder until a pair of horses came to a clattering halt outside the house. Moments later, Tim Hawkins and Chaw Stevens came into the kitchen. Tim had finally relaxed his rule about the hired hands visiting the house.

"Howdy, Miss Nancy," Chaw said, removing his hat.

"Hello, Chaw," Nancy said. She pointed to the pan. "There's a pan full of buttermilk biscuits. Your favorite, if I recall correctly."

"You're sure right about that, Miss Nancy," Chaw said happily. Then he winked at her. "But I think Rawley here likes 'em even better'n me."

"I know for a fact she made these for you, Chaw," Rawley said. He hadn't seen Chaw or Tim since the Cattlemen's Association meeting. "How's things out to the camp?"

Tim poured himself a cup of coffee. "We're all getting edgy. This situation is wrapping itself up."

"That's what Nancy and I was talking about just now," Rawley said.

Tim took a sip of his coffee. "By the way, Pierson. I wanted to say I'm obliged for you taking care o' Nancy the night them bushwhackers hit here. I know you was

173

poorly and you took a chance."

"She got two of 'em herself," Rawley said.

Chaw laughed. "I reckon you two just split 'em up 'tween yourselves, huh?"

"Just the same," Tim said. "Thanks."

"You're welcome," Rawley said.

Tim turned to his sister. "What're we gonna eat with them biscuits?"

"Smoked ham," Nancy said. "Rawley has already sliced it up. It's over on the platter under the cloth."

Tim went over and pulled a piece of the meat out and took a bite of it.

"Tim!" Nancy protested. "That's your supper."

"I ain't eating here," Tim said defending himself. "I'll wolf this down, then go into town."

Nancy started to protest, then changed her mind. "Suit yourself," she said. Tim left and she set the table, motioning to Rawley and Chaw to take seats at the table. After putting the food out, she joined them. "Rawley, will you say grace, please?"

He bowed his head. "We thank you, Lord, for what we're about to eat. Amen."

"Hey," Chaw said. "That's the first time I ever heard you doing something churchy!"

"What'd you think of my prayer?" Rawley asked.

"It wasn't too bad. Maybe you're really a preacher man at heart, Rawley."

Rawley winked at him. "Nancy taught me the words."

"I just hope they mean something to him," Nancy said, eyeing her lover. "Now! Both of you start eating. I went to a lot of work on this meal."

The men ate with gusto, laughing and talking as Chaw brought Rawley up to date on what had been going on at the cattle camp. Nancy, however, remained quiet, responding only when questions or statements

174

were spoken directly to her.

Finally, Rawley asked, "Is there something wrong, Nancy?"

'I don't know," she said. "Tim's card-playing is causing me a lot of worry."

"Is he losing heavy, Miss Nancy?" Chaw asked.

"I think he is because he's not bringing any money home," she said.

"Are you sure he ain't using ranch money?" Rawley asked.

"Yes," she said. "That makes me think he's borrowing heavily."

"He don't sleep out at the camp much," Chaw said. "And when any o' the boys get into town, they always say they see him at the poker table in the Deep River Saloon."

Rawley sighed. "That means he's playing in Big Ed's game with Big Ed's boys."

"Yeah," Chaw agreed. "And with Big Ed's cards too."

"Oh, Rawley!" Nancy exclaimed. "You don't suppose he's being cheated, do you?"

"I don't know," Rawley said. "I never paid much attention to the card-playing in the saloon." He almost reddened when he thought of what he'd done there with Rosalie Kinnon.

"You're one feller that can find out," Chaw said. He looked over at Nancy. "Rawley was perty good with the pasteboards hisself. He knows tricks and ever'-thing. His pa and uncle taught him."

Nancy turned to her fiance. "Darling, could you go into Duncan and watch what's going on? If they're cheating Tim, we've got to put a stop to it."

"You're right about that," Rawley said. "He could be putting the Circle H Bar straight into Big Ed MacWilliams's hands."

175

"Want me to go with you?" Chaw asked.

Rawley shook his head. "Stay here with Nancy. Just in case some o' them range raiders come back."

"Fine with me," Chaw said, taking another look at the good food on the table. He knew there would be enough for a snack later on. "But you be careful, hear?"

"Ain't I always?" Rawley asked.

"No," Chaw answered. "Are we going back to talking about how dumb you can be sometimes?"

Nancy interjected. "Rawley Pierson! Don't do anything foolish!"

"I'll handle things all right," Rawley said. "Don't worry."

"Maybe Chaw should go with you after all," Nancy said.

"It'll be all right," Rawley said. "Now let's finish this delicious supper, and I'll tend to that little matter. The sooner I go, the sooner I get back."

The meal was finished, and Nancy surprised them with an apple cobbler. Chaw, after enduring the bad chuck wagon food for so long, was positively ecstatic as he savored the sweet dessert.

When Rawley finally went out to saddle up for the ride into town, Chaw was still complimenting Nancy on her culinary skill in between bites as he ate his third helping.

The extra amount of fresh air during the ride seemed to increase Rawley's strength even further. By the time he crossed the town limits, he truly felt he was back to normal and that all the infection had been expelled from his system. When he dismounted and tied up his horse in front of the Deep River Saloon, he found Big Ed MacWilliams sitting on the porch as usual. But there was a stranger with him.

"Howdy, Big Ed," Rawley said, walking up.

"Howdy, Pierson," Big Ed said with a stony face.

He nodded to the man beside him. "This here's Cal Witherspoon."

"Howdy," Rawley said. "I'm Rawley Pierson."

Witherspoon, smiling, got out of his chair and walked over to Rawley offering his hand. "I'm most happy to make your acquaintance, sir. I am a former business associate of Ed MacWilliams. I believe he has told you of my consortium's offer to buy up ranch land in this area."

"He's mentioned it, yeah," Rawley said. "But I reckon you've found out that there ain't as much as a square foot o' the Diablos for sale, haven't you?"

"Indeed I have!" Witherspoon said in apparent good humor. "But perhaps someday we can all do mutually beneficial business, hey?"

"Who knows?" Rawley remarked. "Well, pardon me. I been laid up a spell, and I got a need for a good drink o' whiskey."

Rawley went inside the door, and immediately spotted the card game off to one side. He sauntered up to the gaming table and nodded to Tim. "Howdy, Boss. I come in for a drink."

"Is Chaw out to the ranch with Nancy?" Tim asked.

"Yeah," Rawley answered. "She ain't alone."

"Well, I reckon you could use a coupla belts after what you been through," Tim said. "But don't stay long, hear?"

"I gotcha, Boss," Rawley said. He turned to cross the room to the bar and felt an arm slip into his. Rawley smiled. "Howdy, Rosalie."

"I heard you got shot up," she said. "But you look right fine now."

"I need a drink," Rawley said. "C'mon, and I'll buy you one too."

The two went over to the bar, where Roy Patton served them. Rawley took a sip, enjoying the burning

177

sensation of the liquor as he quickly swallowed it. The warmth it made in his belly was pleasurable after so long without whiskey. He glanced over at the game.

"I heard a rumor that you're fianced," Rosalie said.

"Yeah," Rawley replied.

"Is that gonna change any of your habits?" she asked.

"It's gonna change some," Rawley allowed. Then he bluntly added, "Especially where you're concerned."

Rosalie smiled a little sadly. "Oh, Rawley, you'll prob'ly be like all the rest and come in here for us gals after your wife decides she's had enough kids."

"Maybe," Rawley said. He glanced over at the game. "That seems a reg'lar feature in here."

"Almost ever' night," Rosalie said. She looked down the bar to make sure that Patton was out of hearing. "But I'll tell you, Rawley. They're cheating Tim."

"How do you know?"

"I know," Rosalie said. "Nobody has told me nothing outright, but I got a good notion just the same."

"Maybe I should go over and watch the game," Rawley said.

"And maybe you should be careful too," Rosalie warned him. "All the players outside o' Tim are Big Ed's boys."

"I always wondered how many was on his payroll," Rawley said.

"You just watch out," Rosalie said. "This here is a dangerous place for a man like you. That's something else I learned on my own."

"I'll keep an eye out," Rawley promised her. He poured himself another drink, then casually strolled over to the game. "Who's winning?" he asked.

"It ain't me," Tim growled. He called a bet, then laid

178

down his cards. Curly Brandon's full house beat his three of a kind.

Curly swept in his winnings. He glanced up at Rawley. "Care to join in, Pierson?"

Rawley shook his head and affected an innocent grin. "No, thanks. I don't know shit about cards, and anyhow, from the looks o' that pot, I couldn't buy in with a month's wages."

Shorty Clemens laughed. "Anytime you want to learn poker, just look me up. I'll teach you." He laughed again. "O'course I charge for poker lessons."

Rawley chuckled. "By golly, I'll just bet you do."

"Goddamn, Pierson!" Curly said. "I can't believe a feller borned and raised in Texas wouldn't know no more 'bout cards than you say you do."

"I never played, that's all," Rawley said. "I was always nervous when it came to chancing my money."

The game went on. Rawley stayed awhile, then went back to the bar with Rosalie. He returned to the poker table a few more times, watching what was going on in a manner that seemed only mildly curious. But finally, he sat his glass down on the table and stepped back, loosening the gun in his holster.

"You dealt that one off the bottom, Curly," Rawley said in a loud clear voice.

The hum of conversation at the table came to an abrupt halt. A second later, Curly responded. "I think you said something you shouldn't have."

"How about if I say it this way," Rawley offered. "You're cheating at this here card game."

Now Tim leaped to his feet. "Just a goddamn minute Pierson!"

"They're stealing your money, boss," Rawley said, keeping a close eye on Curly. "I don't know how many of the rest of 'em are in on it."

Curly, snarling, grabbed his holster with his left hand and dragged his Colt from it with his right. "You got a big goddamn mouth, Pierson!"

Rawley went for his own iron, a trifle behind Curly, and he instinctively ducked when the other man's pistol blasted at him. By then he was able to return fire, quickly snapping off two shots that missed.

Now Shorty Clemens was in on the gunplay. But he was nervous and fumbled through a slow draw. Curly fired again and missed. His next shot exploded simultaneously with Rawley's. Curly's went past the cowboy's head, but Rawley's bullet hit the cardplayer in the throat.

Now, with blood spurting out of Curly's nose and ears, Shorty Clemens threw out a desperate fusillade that made Roy Patton at the bar dive for cover.

Rawley took deliberate but quick aim and put a killing shot straight into Shorty's chest.

It was over.

Two men lay dead on the floor. Hank Delong and Joe Black kept both hands on the table, giving undeniable evidence they were not going to engage in gunplay.

Big Ed MacWilliams and Calvin Witherspoon came into the room. Big Ed was angry, but wisely said nothing as he noted Rawley standing with a drawn gun.

"My God!" Witherspoon exclaimed. "It's been a hell of a long time since I've seen anything like this."

Sheriff Dan Sims now joined the crowd. He had heard the shooting down at his office. He quickly sized up the situation. "Pierson, put the gun on the table." The sheriff tensed to see what was going to happen.

Rawley looked at Tim, who was staring incredulously at the two dead men. He knew he would have no backup there. "I'm doing like you say, Sims," he said. "Now watch yourself." He slowly reached over and set

180

the pistol down as ordered.

Now Sims pulled his pistol. "You're under arrest for murder," he said to Rawley.

"They drew first," Rawley protested. "I got witnesses."

Sims grinned. "You ain't got shit."

Chapter 19

Calvin Witherspoon stood at the window of his room in Mrs. Malone's boardinghouse. He felt the same nervous apprehension he'd had when he first arrived in the uncertain situation on the Diablos. The New York sharper stared out toward the horizon of the range, knowing that what he was looking at was just a small bit of a gigantic rolling prairie that would someday be worth an incalculable amount of wealth to anyone smart enough, lucky enough, or ruthless enough to gain control of it.

His reverie was interrupted by a knock on the door. "Yes?"

"It's Sheriff Sims," came the answering voice.

"Come in, Sheriff," Witherspoon said.

Sims stepped into the room. He closed the door and leaned against it, giving every indication he wasn't exactly pleased with Witherspoon's summons. His long, thin face wore an expression of near-insolence. "Joe Black says you want to see me."

"Yes, Sheriff," Witherspoon said. "How is the prisoner doing?"

"The prisoner? You mean Rawley Pierson?"

Witherspoon's smile was strained. "Yes, Sheriff. I

mean exactly that. How is Pierson doing?"

"He's been in jail for three days," Sims said. "He's like any man that's been locked up for a spell. But since you seem to need an answer, I'll just say he's getting restless. You didn't call me over here to talk about Pierson, did you?"

Witherspoon ignored the lawman's thinly veiled sarcasm. Something about the rail-thin sheriff made him more leery of him than even of Big Ed MacWillaims. Witherspoon again showed a humble, polite smile. "Actually, I just have a couple of questions, if you don't mind."

"I don't mind," Sims said. "As long as it don't take a lotta time."

"I shall try to be brief. Actually, I was wondering about the procedures for trying Rawley Pierson," Witherspoon said. "It is a most sensitive situation, is it not?"

"I reckon," Sims answered. "I had to go up to the telegraph station at the rail junction and ask for a circuit judge to be sent here to Duncan for the trial. Lucky for us the stage is running. Both him and the prosecutor will be in town this afternoon."

"This is our last chance to get rid of Pierson," Witherspoon said. "If he's acquitted and gets on that cattle drive we can forget all the grand plans for the Diablos."

"I reckon you're right about that," Sims said casually. "We only got three men left out to the hideout. And not only we ain't gonna get more, but they'll be leaving if Pierson ain't took out of the picture. Which he might not be."

"Why the hell not?" Witherspoon demanded to know.

"If we try to hang him, them cowboys will break him free," the sheriff said. "So there ain't no way that he's

183

gonna be dancing at the end of a rope here in Duncan."

"Hell! He's in a cell, isn't he?" Witherspoon asked, exasperated. "Wouldn't it be like shooting fish in a barrel for somebody to get him there?"

"Townfolks is too close," Sims said calmly. "And it's broad daylight."

"Then why didn't you do something last night or the night before?" Witherspoon demanded to know.

"Wasn't necessary," Sims said. "I know this judge."

Witherspoon said nothing for a moment as he stared at the lawman. He was most interested in the direction the conversation seemed to be taking. And he knew it was going to take some effort on his part to get all the information possible out of Sims. "How well do you know him?" he asked.

Sims shrugged. "I've knowed him for a long, long time."

Witherspoon felt a surge of hope. "Can he be—well, persuaded—to see things our way?"

"You mean can we buy him? Sure," Sims said. "But it'll cost at least a thousand."

"What about the prosecutor?"

"Five hundred," Sims said matter-of-factly.

"That's well enough," Witherspoon said. "Now we must worry about the jury."

"Won't be no jury," Sims said. "The judge will declare there ain't enough of folks around that can be fair and square. He'll say he'll make the decision. He'll sentence Pierson to be hung from a rope slung across the cottonwood tree at the end of town. And that'll be before this day's sunset."

Witherspoon shook his head. Sims's conversation was confusing him. "Wait a minute. Even if we get a conviction, you said it wouldn't do any good."

"It will if I have my way," Sims said.

"How?"

184

"Leave it to me," the sheriff assured him. "All we need is to have Pierson sentenced to be hung."

"Damn it, Sims!" Witherspoon said exasperated. "You've told me that would be useless."

"It won't get him hung, but it'll keep him in jail a tad longer," Sims said. He smiled sardonically. "That's all I need. Providing you put up that money I mentioned."

Witherspoon began to understand that Sims had a plan. "In that case I would like to speak to the judge and prosecutor before the trial."

"I'll bring 'em here directly when they arrive," Sims said. "And don't worry about nothing. When the dust all settles and Pierson is gone, we'll get some more hired guns and end that cattle drive to Kansas quick enough."

"If all this works out, I'll see you get some extra compensation," Witherspoon said. "Perhaps we should have put you in charge of this project rather than Ed MacWilliams."

"Maybe you should have, Mister Witherspoon," Sims said. "I'll see you soon." He turned and opened the door, wasting no time in leaving the boardinghouse and getting back to his office.

Witherspoon felt a lot better. The New Yorker had a lot of faith in Sheriff Dan Sims. The man was quiet and observant—a sure sign of shrewdness and determination.

Witherspoon lit one of his cigars and poured some brandy from the bottle he kept in his suitcase. It was an expensive brand he'd brought with him from New York. He even dipped the tip of the cigar in the drink as he enjoyed the small luxury afforded by the smokes and liquor.

After finishing the drink, he stayed in his room only long enough to smoke the cigar to a stub. He flipped the remnants of the tobacco out the window, and went downstairs for a leisurely lunch in the kitchen. He paid Mrs. Malone extra to feed him alone. Although the food in the boardinghouse was far from being gourmet, the woman was a skilled enough cook to make it tolerable to his palate.

After the meal he returned to his room for a brief nap. He'd just gotten to sleep when there was a knock on his door. "Yes?" he called out.

"It's me," Sims said. "I got Judge Carson and Mister Hennesey with me."

Witherspoon almost leaped off the bed. He went to the door and jerked it open. "Come in, please, gentlemen! So good to see you!"

The judge was a short, pudgy man, yet there was no softness about him. His face, though round and almost cherubic, had a quality of cruelty and evil much like that of a half-grown wolf cub. It was easy to see he was no man to be taken lightly if he became angry with someone. His voice was deep and almost bubbly. "We don't have much time. The sheriff tells me that we got a bad hombre to be rid of here."

"Indeed, sir!" Witherspoon said. "My name is Witherspoon."

"Howdy," the judge said.

Next Witherspoon offered his hand to the prosecutor. "I'm Witherspoon."

"Hennesey," the prosecutor said. He was the judge's physical opposite. Tall and gaunt, he had a long face sporting a drooping mustache.

Witherspoon glanced over at Sims. "Since the sheriff is a mutual acquaintance of us all, perhaps it would be best to let him lead this conversation through its logical sequences."

"Pierson is got to be sentenced to be hung," Sims said bluntly. "It's worth a thousand to you, Judge Carson. And five hundred for Hennesey."

Carson glanced at Hennesey. "He'll get a death sentence."

Hennesey nodded.

Witherspoon reached in his coat pocket and withdrew an oil-paper packet. He handed it to the judge. "Fifteen hundred dollars," he announced.

"Yankee dollars, I presume," Carson said taking the package.

"That's the only kind we have in New York State, Your Honor," Witherspoon replied with a slight smile.

Carson turned to the sheriff. "We're wasting time, Dan. Where's the trial to be held?"

"The best place is the Deep River Saloon," Sims answered.

"The Deep River?" Hennesey said with a dry laugh. "There ain't nothing like even a shallow creek in these parts."

"It's a sentimental name for Big Ed MacWilliams," Witherspoon explained. "When he and I were in business in San Angelo he used to speak wistfully of his glory days on the Mississippi."

Carson looked at Witherspoon. "You wouldn't mind telling me why you're so all-fired anxious to hang this Pierson feller, would you?"

"I would," Witherspoon answered.

Carson shrugged and patted the oil-paper packet now in his own coat pocket. "I reckon it makes no never-mind."

Sims opened the door to let the judge and prosecutor leave. He glanced at Witherspoon. "Be down in the saloon in about a half hour."

"I wouldn't miss it for the world," Witherspoon replied. He nodded a farewell to his visitors, then went back to the window to stare out over the Diablos. Once more his mind turned to the value of the sprawling land that lay out before him.

After treating himself to some more brandy and another cigar, he got his hat and left his room, going downstairs. Witherspoon left the boardinghouse and strolled slowly through Duncan to the saloon.

There was plenty of activity around the frame building. Various vehicles with their dumbly patient horses were parked helter-skelter around the main street. The Diablos ranchers and their families lounged on the porch of the Deep River as Witherspoon eased his way through the throng. As a stranger, he was given unabashed stares of open curiosity. He ignored what he considered ill-manner rubes as he went inside. He saw Big Ed MacWilliams, who indicated a chair he was saving for him.

Big Ed grinned. "Sims says it's in the bag."

"Yeah," Witherspoon said. "Just keep your voice down."

"You're a nervous nellie, ain't you, Cal?"

"Damned right! What about those saloon whores of yours?" Witherspoon asked. "They seem to be everywhere—listening and looking. They might queer this whole thing."

"Don't worry," Big Ed assured him. "They been sent away for a while. I got 'em entertaining the boys out at the hideout."

"I'm sure the boys'll appreciate that after all the weeks of staying out on the Diablos," Witherspoon said. He looked around. "There's the prisoner over there."

"That's him all right," Big Ed said. "And I ain't ever seen him looking better."

Rawley Pierson, handcuffed and wearing leg irons, was seated at a chair next to the bar. Near him so they could speak, Nancy Hawkins and Chaw Stevens were doing their best to be cheerful and encouraging.

"Don't you worry none," Chaw told his friend.

188

"This'll be cleaned up in a jiffy. You'll walk through that door a free man ready to make the drive up to Kansas."

Rawley, awkward in the fetters, affected a grin. "I got to tell you something. Being on this side o' the room in a trial is a lot more worrisome than when I was a sheriff."

Nancy smiled. "Never mind, darling. Things will turn out fine just like Chaw says they will."

"Order in the court!" Sheriff Sims shouted out, interrupting the buzz of conversation in the saloon. "This here court is called to order in the name o' the law of the State o' Texas! The honorable Judge P.J. Carson is presiding."

Carson, standing behind the bar, rapped on it with his gavel. "Since there is hard feelings running through town about this case, I'm gonna hereby rule that a trial by jury is waived. It wouldn't be possible to find twelve unprejudiced men. I'll do the deciding."

Rawley spoke up. "I object. I want to have—"

"Objection overruled!" Carson said. He looked over at the prosecutor. "Call your first witness."

"I want Edward MacWilliams to take the stand," Hennesey said.

Big Ed left his chair and walked up to a position beside the bar. He raised his hand at Sims's request and swore to tell the truth, the whole truth, and nothing but the truth.

"Was you here on the night that a man knowed as Shorty Clemens and another knowed as Curly Brandon was killed?" Hennesey asked.

"You bet," Big Ed said.

"Tell us about it."

"I was out at the porch and heard some commotion. I walked in the bar and seen Rawley Pierson there accusing Shorty and Curly of cheating Tim Hawkins at

189

cards," Big Ed said. "They said they hadn't done nothing wrong and then Pierson shot 'em down in cold blood."

"They drawed on me!" Rawley yelled out.

"Order in the court!" Carson shouted. "I ain't putting up with any disturbance, Pierson. You'll have your say."

Rawley quieted down, but his face was still red with anger.

"Did they have their pistols drawed?" Hennesey asked.

"Their irons was in their holsters," Big Ed answered in an outraged tone of voice. "They was murdered in cold blood."

"Thanks for the testimony, Mister MacWilliams," Hennesey said as he dismissed Big Ed. Then he announced, "The next witness is Tim Hawkins."

Chaw leaned forward and whispered in Rawley's ear. "I don't know why the prosecutor is calling him. He'll back up your story."

"Yeah," Rawley agreed. "Since them yahoos was cheating in that game."

Tim was sworn in, then he turned and faced Hennesey. When asked to tell what happened at the card game in question, he said, "I was playing cards with some fellers here, and all of a sudden Rawley Pierson walked up to the table and said that Shorty Clemens and Curly Brandon was cheating me. They got mad and yelled at him, then he shot 'em."

"Did they draw on him, Mister Hawkins?"

"No, sir," Tim answered.

"Was they cheating you at the game?" Hennesey asked.

"No, sir."

"And how do you know that?"

"On account o' I was winning, sir," Tim answered.

190

Hennesey shrugged. "I can't see how you could have been cheated if you was money ahead."

"Me either," Tim answered.

"That's all," Hennesey said. He turned to the judge. "The prosecution rests, Your Honor."

"Thanks, Mister Hennesey," the judge said.

"I'd like to question Tim Hawkins!" Rawley exclaimed.

"I rule against it," Carson said. "But you got a right to testify on your own behalf." He glared at Rawley. "Well? What do you have to say?"

Rawley struggled to his feet. "The first thing I got to say is that this trial ain't being run right," Rawley argued.

"Now how do you know that?" Carson asked.

"I was a sheriff before and seen plenty o' trials," Rawley said.

"Are you a lawyer?"

"Hell, no!" Rawley answered.

"Then don't tell me how to run my court," Carson admonished him.

Rawley knew he was being railroaded. "That bunch was cheating Tim Hawkins. When I was there, he was losing heavy."

"Got any witnesses?" Carson asked.

"Well," Rawley said uncertainly. He looked around. "There was Rosalie Kinnon and Hannah O'Dell. If I could get them, they'd back me up."

"Who are they?" Carson asked.

"They work here," Rawley said.

"They're dance-hall gals, Your Honor," Sims interjected.

"You ain't calling in no lying damned whores in my courtroom!" Carson exclaimed. "Anything else to say?"

"Yeah! I killed them fellers after they drawed on me

191

and they was cheating Tim Hawkins," Rawley said in a rage.

Carson frowned. "You already said that. Don't repeat yourself."

"I don't know why Tim Hawkins said I killed them two in cold blood," Rawley said. "But he's lying!"

Carson banged his gavel. "The defense rests." He took a deep breath. "Two witnesses said Rawley Pierson shot down Shorty Clemens and Curly Brandon in cold blood. One of the witnesses, who was supposed to be getting cheated at cards, says he was coming out winners. That only leaves one verdict. Guilty! And I sentence you, Rawley Pierson, to be took from here day after tomorrow and be hung by the neck till you're dead. Court adjourned!"

Rawley got to his feet in a fury, but the restraints hampered his movements. The ranchers in the saloon kept calm, but their angry grumbling was apparent as Sims grabbed Rawley's arm to take him back to the jail.

Chaw, although his face was drawn and pale with anger, controlled himself. He took Nancy's arm and led the weeping girl from the barroom.

Chapter 20

Big Ed MacWilliams stepped from the stirrups and planted both feet on the ground. Although he appeared determined, a strong sense of uncertainty dominated the large man. For a few moments, he stared up at the Circle H Bar ranch house knowing that Nancy Hawkins was inside. He felt a strange combination of happiness and dread as he thought of the young woman.

Finally, after taking a deep breath to steady himself, Big Ed MacWilliams looped the reins around the hitching rack and walked up on the porch. He knocked on the door. "Miss Nancy?" he called out, peering inside the house's parlor. "Miss Nancy?"

Nancy Hawkins appeared a few moments later. She didn't say anything for a few moments, only glaring at the unwelcome visitor. Finally the young woman said, "I cannot believe you've come here, Mister MacWilliams. Particularly after all the unhappiness that's come to us in your saloon."

"I'm right sorry you feel that way," Big Ed said. "And I ain't surprised about how you think about me. But I wish you would hear me out."

"There is nothing for you to say to me," Nancy said

calmly and coolly.

"I beg your pardon," Big Ed said. He took off his hat and held it in his hands to give an impression of humility. "I feel I have done no wrong toward you nor your'n, Miss Nancy. Most folks would say I don't warrant such a cold treatment as you're showing me now."

"You have condemned the man I intend to marry to the gallows," Nancy said.

"Oh, no! I only told what I seen, as God is my witness," Big Ed said. He rolled his eyes heavenward. "I only wanted to see justice done. And it's writ in the Good Book that's what you're supposed to do."

"How dare you speak of the Holy Bible, sir!" Nancy exclaimed.

Big Ed looked back into her face. "Anyhow, it was the judge that sentenced him to suffer the indignity of a necktie party, not me. And he done what he done legal under the laws of the great State o' Texas."

"Why, oh, why didn't you tell the truth!" Nancy exclaimed. She began to feel she could make Big Ed change his testimony.

"Miss Nancy, I swear to you that Rawley Pierson went into the saloon and drawed on poor ol' Shorty and Curly," Big Ed said. "He shot 'em down in cold blood after accusing 'em of cheating your brother Tim at cards. Them two boys didn't have a chance."

"I believe they were cheating Tim," Nancy said.

"But he was winning," Big Ed said. "Why, Tim is a close friend o' mine, and that's God's truth. Anyhow, when a feller gets cheated, he loses, Miss Nancy. And Tim said hisself that he was raking in the pots. So I reckon that ought to wrap up that argument right proper."

"I haven't had a chance to talk with Tim about the situation," Nancy said. "He's been avoiding me."

"He's prob'ly as heartbroke for you as I am," Big Ed said. He touched his breast in what he hoped was a dramatic gesture. "And I purely feel your pain, Miss Nancy."

"Then go to that judge and tell him what really happened," Nancy insisted. "When Rawley Pierson went to town that night, he did it as a favor to me. There was never any talk of shooting anybody. And he's most certainly not that sort. Rawley has always been a gentleman."

"Oh, Miss Nancy," Big Ed said. "You yourself know that he's a gunman and a former sheriff. Most lawmen is pistoleros at heart. That's why they get into that line o' work. It was only natural for him to walk up to that game and start a gunfight. I bet he done it just 'cause he thought you'd approve of it."

"Then you will not change your testimony, Mister MacWilliams?" Nancy asked.

"Alas!" Big Ed said. He'd heard that used in a play he'd seen in Dallas once. It seemed to fit the scene he was trying to play out. "I cannot! But I am here for a better purpose than to fret over Rawley Pierson's life."

"As far as I'm concerned there is no better purpose, sir!" Nancy cried.

"You must forget him, Miss Nancy, and get on with your own life," Big Ed said. "You've suffered a lot what with your poor old pa getting shot like he did. I want to take you away from this misery, Miss Nancy. I have come to ask you to marry up with me."

"What?"

"Rawley Pierson is a killer!" Big Ed exclaimed. "He ain't good enough for you!" He lowered his voice. "Why, I hate to say this to you, Miss Nancy—seeing as how you're a lady and all—but Rawley Pierson took up with soiled doves in that saloon. One in particular by the name o' Rosalie Kinnon."

195

"I do not believe that, Mister MacWilliams!" Nancy said. "And I'll thank you not to speak of such indelicate matters in my presence."

"Forgive me, please," Big Ed said. "But if I got to talk about the way Rawley Pierson carries on, I can't help but be kinda dirty and low-down like him. And I'm a desperate man. Why I'm a desperado of love, Miss Nancy."

Nancy struggled to control her anger. Finally she said, "Sir, I have no intention of marrying you. And I'll thank you not to set foot on the Circle H Bar again. And if you ever do, I'll shoot you myself!" She slammed the door in his face.

Big Ed stood there for several moments, consumed by rage and disappointment. He'd been turned down by women before, but this was the first time the rejection had been done along with a threat to put a bullet in his hide.

It took a few moments, but he finally got himself under control. He took another calming, deep breath and left the porch, going back to his horse. He swung up into the saddle and looked back at the house. "You'll be proud and happy to become Mrs. Big Ed MacWilliams afore this is all said and done, missy!" he hissed.

Big Ed pulled on the reins of his horse and galloped out of the ranch yard. He knew exactly where to find Tim Hawkins.

The young man, wanting very much to avoid both Nancy's company and the cattle camp where the cowboys and Chaw Stevens would be, had fixed himself a bivouac of sorts among a stand of cottonwoods located between the ranch and the town. There was every chance that he might be the one dangling from a rope if a lynching got on the drovers' collective minds.

Tim had drunk himself insensible that first night, and was now terribly hungover as he sat around the embers of fire where a pot of coffee boiled with gurgling bubbles.

When he heard a horse approaching, he stood up to see who it was. After spotting Big Ed MacWilliams, Tim sat back down and went back to staring at the campfire.

Big Ed reined up and quickly dismounted. "I'm glad to see you ain't cut out for some faraway place. I ain't done with you yet."

Tim looked up at him. "For the love o' God, Big Ed! What more could you want of me?"

"I ain't asked for half o' what I could get outta you," Big Ed said. "And don't you forget it!"

"I asked you what more do you want," Tim said sullenly. "I ain't in a mood to put up with threats."

"I'm dead set on marrying your sister," Big Ed said.

"She won't have you," Tim said.

"That's for you to change," Big Ed said.

"How?"

"You might start by telling her it's the only way you're gonna keep that goddamned ranch," Big Ed said.

"What the hell are you talking about?" Tim yelled. He leaped to his feet. "I lied for you at the trial. You said that'd wipe out all them IOUs. I don't owe you one goddamned cent, Big Ed." He suddenly calmed down and laughed. "Hell! You even give 'em to me. I tore 'em up."

"I didn't give *all* of 'em to you, you dumb sonofabitch," Big Ed said with a grin. "I still got enough paper on you to take two or three of them Circle H Bars. And your signature is on ever' one of 'em."

Tim's hand dropped to his pistol. "You low-down—"

Big Ed whipped a derringer from inside his coat. "Don't try playing the gunman with me, boy! I faced down more men than you can imagine, and shot my share too."

Tim lifted his hand away from the weapon. He knew he'd been driven into a deep hole with no way out. "Have your say."

"Aside from making me your brother-in-law, you're also gonna let me know what them ranchers are up to," Big Ed said. "You'll go to their association meetings and listen to ever'thing they plan to do. Then you'll tell me all about it, understand?"

"What the hell do you care about what the ranchers has got up their sleeves?" Tim asked.

"I got a personal interest in what happens here on the Diablos," Big Ed said. "I want them Easterners to buy up this territory."

Tim's face paled. "Are you behind them raiders? The ones that killed my pa?"

Big Ed grinned crookedly. "You don't ask *me* questions, boy! For all intents and purposes I already own the Circle H Bar."

Tim almost vomited with rage. But something deep inside his being told him that this was not the time or place to make any plays. Although visibly shaken, he stood there, teeth clenched, looking at the other man.

Big Ed got back up on his horse. "Take care, Tim Hawkins. You ain't in no position to get sassy or mean. And if you want to avoid further misery, you'll do exactly as I say." He swung the horse around and kicked it into a gallop as he headed back for the town of Duncan.

The ride from the campsite was less than a half hour. Big Ed didn't go to the Deep River Saloon. Instead he went directly to the jail. Once there, he went inside to speak with Sheriff Dan Sims.

Sims stood at the door leading to the cells. He kept a wary eye on the prisoner, Rawley Pierson, when Big Ed came into the office. "What's up?" Sims asked.

"I got to talk to you," Big Ed said.

"Let's make it quick," Sims said. He withdrew into the interior of the room and lowered his voice. "I got plans for Pierson."

"That's what I come to find out," Big Ed said. "I ain't heard nothing since you got so all-fired chummy with that sonofabitch Witherspoon."

"You don't tell me my business, Ed," Sims said. "I'll deal with who I want, won't I?"

Big Ed eased down. "Sure, Dan. I didn't mean nothing. I'm just worried, that's all."

"I got definite plans worked out," Sims said.

"What's going on?" Big Ed asked.

"Well, I reckon you've also figured out that it's too risky to try a hanging tomorrow," Sims said. "Them cowpokes is gonna come in from the Diablos and put an end to it."

"Are you gonna string him up sooner?" Big Ed asked.

"I ain't gonna string him up at all," the lawman replied. "Rawley Pierson is gonna get shot trying to escape tonight."

"I don't follow you," Big Ed said puzzled. "But I gotta admit I like the direction you seem to be headed."

"I'm gonna make a deal with the bastard," Sims explained. "I'll tell him it'd serve ever'body's purpose best if he just got off the Diablos and stayed off. I'll tell him that if he agrees to leave, I'll let him walk outta here. I already got his horse tied up in back to convince him."

"Why not just shoot him now?" Big Ed said. "You can tell the townfolks that he jumped you."

"Nobody but a damn fool would try to escape a jail

199

in a town like this in broad daylight," Sims explained. "And I reckon most folks around here know that Pierson has a lot o' savvy. If he was to try a break, it'd be at night."

"I reckon you're right," Big Ed allowed.

"Hell, yes, I'm right!" Sims insisted. "Leave it to me. I'll get him afore he's gone a half-dozen steps past the back door."

"It'll be dark," Big Ed cautioned him. "Suppose you miss."

"I brought in the boys from the hideout," Sims said. "They're scattered around town and can cover any place Pierson might run off to."

"I'll be ready at the saloon," Big Ed said. "Hank Delong and Joe Black can be standing by too."

"Pierson ain't got a chance," Sims said. "Why don't you get on back to the Deep River now? I'll start this thing rolling with Pierson."

Big Ed nodded. He went to the door and waved back with a wink before going out into the street.

Sims walked back to his position by the door. He looked in at Rawley sitting handcuffed and shackled in his cell. The sheriff grinned. "How'd you like to get them things took off?"

Rawley looked up at him. "Sure. Send out for some fried chicken and dumplings too while you're at it."

"I ain't joshing you, Pierson," Sims said. "I'm willing to get you outta them irons."

"I bet."

"And outta this jail too," Sims added.

"You're fixing to do that when you hang me in the morning, ain't you?"

"Maybe a hanging ain't necessary," Sims said. "Maybe it'd be best for ever'body if you managed to get away from here tonight."

Rawley displayed a quizzical look. "What're you

200

getting at, Sims?"

"C'mon, Pierson," Sims said. "They ain't nobody here but you and me. You know we skunked you. And Tim Hawkins knows we skunked you too."

"That won't make no differ'nce to me when I'm swinging on that tree out there," Rawley said.

"I said that might not be a good thing," Sims said. "Especially if Tim Hawkins gets a twinge o' conscience. He might think things over and come riding in here tomorrow and save you by telling the truth."

"And maybe he won't," Rawley said.

"That's a chance we don't want to take," Sims said. "And what if he starts yapping away a few weeks or months from now? That'll still mean big trouble around here."

"I reckon so," Rawley said.

"So what if I let you ride outta here tonight, will you just keep a-going?"

"Damn right I will!"

"I already got your horse out there," Sims said. "He's all saddled and ready to go. Hop over to the window and take a gander."

Rawley struggled to his feet. He made his way over to the barred opening and looked out. "I reckon you're telling the truth. You let me walk outta here tonight, Sims, and I swear to you that I'll ride like the wind and never come back on the Diablos. You can count on that."

"I am," Sims said. He pulled the keys off his belt. "Now let me get you outta them irons like I said I would."

Chapter 21

Rawley Pierson lay on the bunk in the cell. Wide-awake and nervous, he rubbed his wrists where the cruel handcuffs had pinched his flesh for long hours. It was a relief to be rid of not only the iron confinements that had bound his hands, but also the shackles from around his ankles. But that improvement in his physical comfort did nothing to help his patience.

He still felt agitated and apprehensive, even after the conversation with Sheriff Dan Sims. Chaw had come to visit him the previous night, staying in the shadows as the two whispered back and forth while Rawley kept a sharp eye and ear out for any intrusion by his keeper.

Chaw had assured him that there would be no hanging. The ranchers and cowboys would come to town to prevent that. The cowmen were too grateful for all the help Rawley had given them to allow him such a terrible and ignoble death.

While the knowledge of any potential rescue by his friends gave Rawley deep feelings of relief, he feared the bloodshed that could result from any rash actions. The lives of some mighty nice folks might get snuffed out. And it would all be on his account. Rawley didn't know if he could live with that or not.

Then Sims had offered him that way out. But since talking to Sheriff Dan Sims, the time had seemed to crawl along endlessly. His mood swung between elation and depression as the hours dragged by in the Duncan town jail.

Now it was dark outside, and the moon slid out from behind the clouds and threw a bright light on that edge of the big, wide Diablos Range. The noise in the Deep River Saloon had finally quieted down, and Rawley guessed the time to be a bit past midnight. A noise in the office caught his attention and he looked toward the door.

Sheriff Dan Sims stepped into the cell block. "Well, Pierson. Do you feel rabbity?"

"I do," Rawley answered getting to his feet.

Sims opened the barred door. He handed Rawley's gunbelt and pistol to him. "Remember your promise. Get the hell out of Duncan and off the Diablos and stay off. Right?"

"Right!"

"It wouldn't be a bad idea if you cleared Texas altogether," Sims suggested. "That might save a lotta folks plenty o' trouble. And that goes double for your pals on the ranches."

"Me and Chaw was headed for New Mexico when we come here," Rawley said. "I reckon that's the best place to go."

"Well, you write to your old pal and tell him where you are when you get there," Sims warned him. "When I said to vamoose, I meant *now*. I don't want you waiting around for Chaw Stevens."

"Sure," Rawley said. He quickly buckled on his weapon. He pulled the pistol, noting the lightness of its weight. "My iron's empty."

Sims grinned. "Damn right. I ain't no fool, Pierson. You might be having bad feelings toward me. Know

203

what I mean?"

"I sure do," Rawley said. "Well, so long, Sims. It ain't been nice knowing you."

"Likewise," Sims replied.

Rawley turned and walked toward the door leading to the outside. He opened it and looked out, surveying the scene. "I don't see nobody."

"There ain't supposed to be nobody," Sims said. He eased his pistol from its holster and aimed dead on Rawley Pierson's back.

A pistol blasted, lighting up the cells.

Sims gasped and staggered back, dropping his Colt. Chaw Stevens stepped inside, his smoking gun in his right hand. He held a Winchester carbine in his left. "Surprise, you lying backshooting bastard!"

The sheriff stumbled sideways into the wall and slid down it into a sitting position. "Goddamn it!" he gasped.

"I was squatting outside the jail there and Rawley told me about the deal you offered him. You must really think we're stupid, Sims," Chaw said. "We didn't believe for a minute that you'd turn him a-loose. You got more to gain by killing Rawley than trusting him to leave the Diablos. So it seemed smart for me to be here as a backup."

Rawley busily loaded his own pistol from the bullets in his gunbelt. "Did you bring my carbine?"

"This is it," Chaw said, tossing the weapon to his friend. "Now we better make a beeline outta here."

"Get me some help, boys," Sims pleaded in a weak voice.

"Piss up a rope," Chaw said.

"There ain't no help anyhow," Rawley pointed out. "You know Duncan ain't got a doctor."

Sims sighed and breathed shallowly. "I'm hurting, boys."

"I'll bet you are!" Rawley said coldly. "I reckon taking a shot in the chest like that ought to hurt just about anybody."

"C'mon, Rawley!" Chaw urged him.

Rawley took another look at the sheriff, noting the glazed stare that had come in his eyes. The end had come fast. "He's cashed in, Chaw."

"Good riddance." Chaw led the way out the door, then quickly jumped back in. "There's a crowd gathering."

"Don't worry about it," Rawley said. "If they're from the saloon they're drunk. And if they just got outta bed to see what the hell's going on, they ain't thinking any clearer than the drinkers. Follow me."

He rushed past Chaw and went outside, his pistol barking fire and slugs in the air in an effort to discourage any onlookers from forming an impromptu posse. Chaw followed. The pair rushed to their horses and vaulted into the saddles at the same time that a fusillade of shots cut the air around them and slapped into the jailhouse.

"Them boys ain't drunk!" Chaw yelled.

"Sonofabitches!" Rawley said. "I'll bet they're part o' the gang. They musta been out here waiting in case I got away from Sims. He was smart enough to have some backups in case something went wrong with his plans."

"If they're the raiders, that means Sims was in on that land grab," Chaw said.

"We ain't got time to talk about it now," Rawley said pulling on the reins. "Ride!"

They headed northward, but only got about fifty yards before they attracted more six-gun attention. Swinging to the west while returning fire, Rawley and Chaw urged their horses into a gallop as they made a wild dash through the town. When they gained the open country of the Diablos, they dug their spurs in and rode for their lives. Knowing that an organized pursuit followed them added to their desperation.

By then the moon was out in full, giving an almost daylight exposure to the flat, rolling prairie country of the range. Rawley glanced back, and could see a half dozen riders after them. He knew it was useless to shoot at them. Only an impossibly lucky shot would hit any of the pursuers. Like Chaw, he rode on doggedly, sticking to the saddle in the bouncing, wild gallop across the Diablos.

Their horses strained to meet the demand in the bid for freedom, but the weeks of working the cattle herd had left the animals unfit for a long, continuous gallop. The only hope Rawley and Chaw had was for the mounts to last long enough to get to a place where they could at least stop and defend themselves until help arrived from the cowboys. Trying a standoff where they now rode would be suicide. No cover, no defense, and no luck but bad.

Chaw, his voice distorted by the bouncing ride, shouted, "We can—last maybe—another half—hour and—that's all!"

Rawley pointed to their right front. "Dips—in the ground—and scrub brush—shadows!"

They turned in that direction and galloped into uneven ground that was dangerous for riding. Having nothing to lose, they twisted and turned in the saddle as the horses dodged the shadowy obstacles of vegetation and ground swells. But at least it forced the more wary chasers to slow down their pace.

Suddenly a lone rider appeared on the horizon. He reined to a halt as Rawley and Chaw closed in on him. Both hoped it would be one of the cowpokes who might be a vanguard of others on their way into town for the hanging. When they drew up beside him and halted,

206

they saw it was Tim Hawkins.

"What're you doing outta jail, Pierson?" Tim asked.

Rawley quickly realized that the young man wasn't in on his planned murder in a phoney jail break. "We got a gang o' them raiders on our asses," he said, drawing his Colt. "Now you make a decision whether to help or not. And you do it *now!*"

"And Sims is in with 'em," Chaw added.

"So is Big Ed MacWilliams," Tim said. He glanced outward. "They're coming closer, boys. There's a draw over that way. Get into it and stay down."

"How do we know you won't turn us over to 'em?" Chaw asked.

"I just got the facts figgered out myself, Chaw!" Tim exclaimed hotly. "They killed my pa. Now get to that draw!"

Forced to trust Tim Hawkins, Rawley and Chaw did as he instructed. They found a natural cut in the earth no more than a yard deep. But the sagebrush growing along its edge gave them cover in the moonlight.

The pursuers, led by Hank Delong and Joe Black, drew up in front of Tim Hawkins. Joe stood in his stirrups and looked around while Hank asked, "Have you seen Pierson and that old galoot pard o' his come this way?"

"What'd Pierson do? Break outta jail?" Tim asked, trying to put a tone of surprise in his voice.

"Sure did," Joe Black said interjecting. "And prob'ly killed Sims too."

"Well?" Hank asked. "You seen 'em or not?"

"Yeah. I seen 'em, all right," Tim answered. He pointed toward the north. "They was headed for Rattlesnake Arroyo where the cattle camp is."

"Goddamn, boys!" Joe Black exclaimed. "If they meet up with them cowboys, our game is up. We gotta catch 'em and do it quick!"

The half-dozen riders lurched back into a gallop, leaving Tim alone on the prairie. He watched them go, then shouted out, "They're all gone. Come on back up."

Rawley and Chaw came out of the draw. Chaw came straight to the point. "What's your game, kid?"

"I'm gonna set things straight," Tim said. "I didn't know that Big Ed was part o' the raiders gang."

"You found that out?" Rawley asked.

"Yeah. That means he had a hand in killing my pa," Tim said. "I thought about it, and got so riled I couldn't stand it. I finally calmed down enough to get myself ready for a showdown."

"Back off, kid," Chaw said coldly.

"You're good with your fists, but you ain't no gunfighter yet," Rawley cautioned him. "You better join up with us if you want to bring this thing to a head."

Tim was thoughtful for a moment. "You're right. Anyhow, like I said, I figgered out Big Ed and them bushwhackers have been working for his old pal Witherspoon. I went to the ranchers and told 'em ever'thing. Even about lying at your trial, Pierson."

"They didn't believe you, did they?"

Tim shook his head. "They called me a damn liar. They said I was trying to cover up. They're convinced you really gunned them boys down and the judge sentenced you legal to hang. But they're planning on coming in later to let you loose anyhow."

"We can't wait around for 'em to show up," Rawley said. "We wouldn't last a minute if more of Big Ed's boys come around."

"Let's get the hell outta Texas," Chaw said. "There ain't no way that judge and prosecutor is gonna swear out warrants on us. They'll be happy as hell to be done with this whole thing."

208

"That's the easy way," Rawley said. "I got Nancy to take care of. I ain't leaving her."

"Then if you ain't leaving, you're gonna have to fight," Chaw said. "And you'll need help. From what Tim says, you can't count on the ranchers for a while. And you ain't got a while, old pal. Maybe Jim Pauley and Duane Wheeler will sneak away early and come into town."

Rawley shook his head. "We can't count on that. But there's one sure thing we can do. If we get rid o' Big Ed and Witherspoon, we'll win the range war. They're the ones paying the freight on this Diablos affair."

"You're right," Chaw agreed. "And it'll be easy for us to take them two."

"It'll be more'n them," Tim cautioned them. "The whole gang didn't chase you. There's 'bout three or four more of 'em that stayed in town." He took a deep breath. "I reckon I was loco to figger on riding into Duncan alone. So I'm going in with you."

"I ain't seen you in much action," Rawley said. "You was usually in town playing cards and drinking when the raiders hit."

"Yeah," Chaw said. "Do you think you can lend a fair hand in a shootout?"

Tim nodded. "I won't back down one way or the other. I'm Zeb Hawkins' son."

"That's good enough for me," Rawley said.

"How're we gonna do it, Rawley?" Chaw asked.

"We'll go directly back, but circle around and come in from the opposite end o' town," Rawley said. "Then we go to the Deep River and do what's got to be did."

"It ain't gonna be that easy," Tim said. "Big Ed's got his town boys on guard. They'll see us."

"Then it's gotta be fast," Rawley said. "If they hold us up, these jaspers that was chasing us will come back and then we'll really be in deep shit."

209

"Big Ed won't go down easy," Tim said. "He's handy with a gun too. I seen him gun down a crazed cowboy when the feller was all likkered up and shooting up the saloon."

"This job seems to get tougher all the time," Rawley said.

"Let's get it did!" Chaw urged him.

"I'm doing this for Nancy and Tim is doing it for the Circle H Bar," Rawley said. "You got nothing to gain here, Chaw. Nobody expects you to stick around. You oughta head on off to Delbert's place in New Mexico where we was going in the first place."

"And you oughta shut your damn mouth and ride," Chaw said. "Let's go, boys." Without waiting, the old man spurred his horse into action and began a fast ride back toward Duncan.

Whipping their reins, Rawley Pierson and Tim Hawkins followed after him.

210

Chapter 22

The moon lit up Duncan, Texas, as Rawley Pierson crept through the sagebrush just outside the town limits. In spite of the brightness, the shadows cast by the buildings still offered a good deal of cover and concealment.

Rawley glanced to his right, and could see Chaw advancing alongside about twenty yards way. Tim Hawkins was situated similarly on the left. Signaling at them now and then to keep the alignment correct, Rawley led them up to the small business district, then turned and made his way past the back of the stores. At this point he emitted a low whistle and gestured to his companions. The pair closed up on him at that point, and they all slowly moved through the shadows with their six-guns at the ready.

"Hold it!" Rawley hissed. "There's a light in the Deep River Saloon."

Tim nodded. "Yeah. It looks like Big Ed and his boys have decided to stay up for the night's events."

"This is gonna make it a tad harder to get 'em, ain't it," Chaw commented.

"I suppose it would. I reckon we can't sneak up on 'em very easy now. But that adds to the fun," Rawley said with raw humor. "Particular when you keep in mind that they're wide awake and armed."

"Well, sleeping or awake, we ain't gonna get 'em by standing around and jawing out here," the older man said.

Tim said, "There's a storeroom in the back of the Deep River. It's where they keep beer barrels and crates o' whiskey bottles."

"In that case, I think we're better off going through the rear of the saloon," Rawley said. "They'll all be in the barroom and we can throw down on 'em there."

"Yeah," Tim agreed nervously. "They're probably just sitting around playing cards or drinking."

Rawley again took the lead as the trio approached the rear of the Deep River. When they reached it, he checked the back door and found it unlocked. After he eased it open, Rawley, Chaw, and Tim stepped inside, walking gingerly into a storeroom that was exactly as Tim had described it.

"This is too easy," Chaw whispered. He chuckled softly. "We'll have this thing wrapped up and tied with a perty red bow in about another fifteen minutes."

"Get ready," Rawley said. "On my word, we'll—"

The door opened and Roy Patton, the bartender, stepped inside. He'd gone no more than three steps toward the barrel of beer he was after when he spotted the intruders.

"Big Ed!" he shouted, turning and rushing out. "Pierson and Tim Hawkins is in there with the old fart."

"Old fart?" Chaw yelled out in stunned indignation.

Before he could make any more comments, shooting broke out in the main room and the slugs crashed through the thin plank wall, flying around Rawley and his friends.

212

They instinctively returned fire as they backed out of the building. But when they reached the alley, more shots came their way from two of Big Ed's men who had run around side of the saloon. A retreat in the opposite direction was cut off by the sudden appearance of three more pistoleros who had scrambled to cover that area.

Rawley and Chaw instinctively turned toward the lesser number and kicked out several shots in the pistoleros' direction. One of the men crumpled to the ground while the other beat a hasty withdrawal back around the building. This time it was Chaw ahead of his friends as they rushed past the place and continued down to the blacksmith shop.

"Is there a back door?" Chaw asked looking at the unfamiliar building.

"I don't think so," Tim called out from the rear.

"Then where do you want one?" Chaw asked. He slammed against the building with his boot, trying to break into the frame wall.

"Don't be loco, Chaw!" Rawley shouted. Now he went to the front and found the large doors there. There was only a hasp holding them shut. Rawley yanked it open and the three went inside. They came to a panting halt, standing close together in the darkness of the building.

"Well, now, ain't we accomplished a lot?" Chaw mused. "We had a chance to be on our way free and clear to New Mexico, but we come back here so's we could get cornered in a blacksmith shop."

"That was part of my clever plan," Rawley said, grinning as he reloaded his pistol.

"You *planned* this?" Chaw inquired.

"Well, not the whole thing," Rawley allowed. "Just the part about coming into town."

Tim didn't appreciate the older ones' banter while they all faced death. He peered out between a crack in the boards. "Do you reckon they know where we are?" he asked.

A volley of shots exploded from outside, smacking into the building.

"Does that answer your question?" Chaw inquired.

"Maybe we're better off in here," Tim suggested.

Rawley wasn't so optimistic. "I don't think so. All this shooting is gonna wake up the townfolks. They'll be joining in on the side o' Big Ed and his boys. Don't forget that they figger I'm a cold-blooded killer."

"Yeah," Chaw said. "Thanks to Tim here."

"Let's not go into that," Rawley said. "We could be facing a small army in another quarter or half hour."

"Well, this is a hell of a mess we're in, ain't it?" Tim complained.

More shots crashed into the building as if to emphasize his statement.

"We're gonna have to act fast, boys," Rawley said.

"What've you got in mind?" Chaw asked.

"If you want to kill a rattlesnake, you chop off his head, don't you?" Rawley said. "And that's what I intend to do."

"You're gonna get Big Ed and forget the rest o' these bushwhackers for the time being?"

"I sure as hell am. He'll be back in the saloon," Rawley said. "I want you boys to set up a hell of a lot of shooting to make them jaspers out there duck their heads and be a little more nervous and respectful. While they're blinking their eyes, I'll go out that window yonder and make my way in the shadows up the alley."

"Gun down Big Ed outright, Rawley," Chaw urged him. "He's a sneaky sonofabitch."

214

"I'll do what looks best at the time," Rawley said. "Now start shooting, boys."

Chaw and Tim each eased up to one of the windows. Chaw licked his lips once and said, "Now!"

Their two six-guns spit fire and lead as Rawley took advantage of the distraction to slip through a side window. He dropped down to the ground and rapidly crawled around the blacksmith shop to the back. Then, staying in the shadows, he got to his feet and hurried down the alley.

After going a few yards, Rawley halted and waited. A flurry of firing broke out back where Chaw and Tim still held out, but it died down. The knowledge that there wasn't much time to waste spurred Rawley back into action. He hurried past the general store, and tensed up as he neared the saloon.

A gunman suddenly appeared from the darkness between the buildings and swung his carbine hard at Rawley. The blow hit him on the shoulder, although it was really meant for his head.

The attack was a glancing strike, but it was on his recently injured shoulder. Rawley's right arm went numb, and he dropped his pistol as he stumbled and went to his knees. But he managed to regain his feet and turn to see the man take another swing at him with the carbine. The hired gun had evidently been in the midst of reloading when Rawley passed his hiding place. Rawley ducked again as the heavy barrel missed him by scant inches. He tried to pick up the Colt, but his fingers couldn't grasp the weapon.

The gunman, in a furious frenzy, tried once more. Rawley dropped down again, hearing the whistling sound of another near miss go past his ears. But this time, using his left hand, he managed to get the pistol. Normally right-handed, he held the Colt in his left, feeling clumsy and awkward.

"Goddamn you!" the man cussed desperately in his effort to brain Rawley. He took another vicious swipe with the Winchester. "I'll bash your skull into bits!"

Desperate and fast running out of time, Rawley had no choice but to fire fast before he got his head caved in. The slug crashed into the man's lower jaw, lifting him free of the ground. Thanking whatever lucky stars he had, Rawley was already at a dead run toward the saloon door before the unlucky bushwhacker hit the ground in a knee-buckling thud.

Knowing the last shot would have attracted attention in the lull of the gunfight, Rawley could no longer depend on guile or concealment to see him through. He pushed through the back door of the Deep River Saloon, sped across the storeroom, and burst out into the main barroom.

The first man who turned toward him was the bartender, Roy Patton. The man had a scattergun, but he only had time to turn the double barrels toward Rawley before one of two snap shots took him down with a chest wound.

Rawley whirled to face the next opposition, but there was nobody there but Rosalie Kinnon. She stared at him nervously, then suddenly shouted, "Rawley! Up on the stairs!"

He whirled and saw Big Ed MacWilliams just as the saloon owner fired his .44 Smith and Wesson. The bullet whistled by Rawley's head. Firing left-handed was more difficult at this longer range. Rawley's shot missed at the same time that Big Ed tried again. That slug kicked up splinters in the floor between Rawley's feet. Rawley desperately let off two more shots as he backed toward the cover of the bar.

But one of the slugs found the target.

Big Ed lurched backward and grabbed the bannister. Standing unsteadily, he raised the pistol again. But Rawley also was taking careful aim. Using the numb right hand as a rest under the barrel, he squeezed the trigger in a desperate hope for a second hit.

The .45-caliber hunk of lead slammed into Big Ed's sternum, rocking him back on his heels. The saloon owner made a final effort to fire, but died on his feet and tumbled down the stairs to end up crumpled across the bottom steps.

Rawley turned to Rosalie. "Is there anyone—"

The girl lay across the table, her blood spreading out to the edge and dripping down on the floor. One of Big Ed's bullets had hit her. She gasped and struggled to get up, but failed.

Rawley rushed to her, and picked her up to carry her to the bar, where he laid her down. "Easy, gal," he said softly, trying to make her comfortable.

"Witherspoon . . ." She spoke with a great effort. "Upstairs with . . . Hannah . . ." That was all she said. Her death rattle was no more than a gentle sound coming from her throat.

Rawley, reloading as he ascended the stairs, went directly to the other dance-hall girl's room. He kicked the door open and started to fire.

"Don't shoot!" Witherspoon begged. He dropped to his knees and held out his hands in a begging gesture. "For the love of God, don't kill me—please! I'm not armed! I swear to God, Pierson! I'm not armed!"

"Lemme outta this goddamned place!" Hannah shouted. She rushed out the door, then yelled out when she saw Rosalie's body. "Oh, God in heaven!"

"Come on, Witherspoon," Rawley said. "If you don't want to get shot, don't try to be cute. Get on your feet. We're going down to the blacksmith's place and put an end to the gunplay."

"Sure, Pierson. Anything you say," Witherspoon said. He smiled in an ingratiating way as he got off his knees. "This can all be put right. You're not going to shoot me, are you?"

"If you don't do what I say, I damned well will," Rawley snarled.

"Let's not get excited, please!" Witherspoon pleaded.

"I'm already excited, goddamn your eyes. Now *move!*"

They stepped out into the street and moved down toward the sound of firing with Witherspoon walking in front of the fugitive. Rawley noted that now several men from the town were behind cover while taking occasional shots at the blacksmith shop.

Rawley slapped Witherspoon hard across the back of his shoulders. "Tell 'em to knock off the shooting."

"Hold it!" Witherspoon hollered.

"Louder," Rawley commanded.

"Everybody stop firing," Witherspoon yelled with more gusto. "Don't shoot at the men in the blacksmith shop anymore!"

The firing slowly died off. Then Rawley yelled, "Tim! C'mon out and give these folks the truth."

Moments later, the door to the building was pushed open and Tim stepped out. Several exclamations of surprise at seeing him were uttered by the locals. Tim spoke loudly. "Listen to me! I lied at the trial. Rawley Pierson didn't shoot down Curly and Shorty like I said. They drawed on him first."

One of the townsmen, the owner of the general store, was puzzled. "How come you did that, Tim?"

"I owed Big Ed money and he made a deal with me," Tim said. "I'm shamed to say so, but I lied. That's why

I joined back up with Rawley and Chaw to set things right."

Now Chaw appeared. "You heard him. So let's simmer down and do it fast afore somebody nice around here gets hurt. That'd be a shame since Tim just spoke you the truth."

"And there's more to the story," Tim said. "Big Ed MacWilliams and his old pal Witherspoon have been trying to run off the ranchers on the Diablos. They killed my pa. I just found that out."

Rawley nudged Witherspoon. "Well, you dandy dude! Back him up!"

"Tim Hawkins is speaking the truth," Witherspoon said. "Sheriff Sims was part of the scheme as well."

"Where's Big Ed?" one of the pistoleros yelled out.

"He's dead," Witherspoon answered.

The surviving two hired gunmen became agitated and nervous. They instinctively drew off together toward the general store. With the townspeople now armed, having tried to recapture what they thought was an escaped killer, the situation showed every promise of turning nasty for them. One of the gunmen shouted, "We're pulling out. If anybody tries to stop us or come after us, they're dead!"

The townspeople, confused and uncertain, did nothing to stop them. The pair quickly disappeared into the darkness, and were quickly gone.

"Want us to go after 'em, Rawley?" Chaw shouted.

"Let 'em go," Rawley said. At the point he considered it good riddance. A forced showdown would end in unnecessary bloodshed. Rawley saw no sense in adding any Duncan citizens to the list of people who'd died in the Diablos Range War. At any rate, there was another way to deal with the escapees.

"Ever'body down to the saloon," Rawley yelled.

"We'll wrap this up."

Within fifteen minutes, the saloon was filled with townspeople. Rosalie Kinnon's body was carried away, but Big Ed MacWilliams still sprawled on the bottom of the stairs. Rawley addressed the crowd. "Now listen to Tim Hawkins. He's got the whole story on what's been happening on the Diablos."

Tim quickly explained the land-grab scheme, and told of Big Ed MacWilliams and Witherspoon's parts as masterminds. He again confessed to perjury in Rawley's trial, and told of how the judge and prosecutor had been bribed by Witherspoon. When he finished, all the Duncan citizens were silent for a few moments with shock and surprise.

"There's some more o' them hired guns out on the Diablos with Hank Delong and Joe Black," Rawley said. "They're looking for me and Chaw. Them two pistoleros that just lit out are pals o' theirs. That means that whole bunch will be on their way to Mexico before this morning's sun is over the horizon. But they'll never make it. Somebody from town can make a quick trip up the rail junction and send a telegraph to the Texas Rangers. A few of those boys will be enough to take care o' them." He grabbed Witherspoon's arm. "And we got the big cheese right here anyhow."

The owner of the general store, who acted as mayor, stepped forward. "Mister Pierson, it seems we need to see to Duncan's law and order. As I recall from things I heard, you and Chaw Stevens served as law officers down south. Would y'all be available as sheriff and deputy?"

Rawley shrugged and smiled. "Well—"

Tim interrupted. "Hell, no, they ain't available. You're talking to my foreman here. And Chaw Stevens is the Circle H Bar's top hand."

220

"I always knowed I was," Chaw said.

"The boss is right," Rawley said. "And we got a cattle drive to get moving by tomorrow at this time." He grabbed Witherspoon's arm again. "But I will lock this skunk up. Have you got somebody to watch the jail till more law gets called in to Duncan?"

"Sure," the mayor said. "Looks like we're gonna have another trial."

"Just keep him in the calaboose till we get back from Kansas," Chaw said. "Then you'll see justice did around here, by God!"

Chapter 23

The loud voices of cussing cowboys intermingled with the bawling of cattle as the herd moved out of Rattlesnake Arroyo and back up on the flatter ground of the Diablos. Dust kicked up by hundreds of hooves rose into the air, growing thick as the herd was urged into motion by the impatient drovers.

All the Diablos ranches were represented by the group of drovers—the Circle H Bar, Lazy S, Diamond T, Double Box, and Flying Heart—and the communally owned cattle now moved out under their combined guidance and skills.

Rawley Pierson rode a bit to the outside, keeping an eye on Chaw Stevens, Jim Pauley, and Duane Wheeler as they wheeled their horses into the formation. He glanced over at Doak Timmons, owner of the Diamond T. The night before, the ranchers had elected him as the overseer of the cattle drive.

Rawley shouted, "The Circle H is in position, Mister Timmons."

"That's ever'body then," Timmons yelled back. "Okay, boys. Let's get these dogies up to Kansas. Move 'em out!"

Whistles and yells erupted now, and the cattle began

moving northward in a route that would take them off the Diablos and onto the trail to Dodge City.

Tim Hawkins galloped up to Rawley and reined in. He grinned. "You ain't said your final good-byes yet, have you?"

"Another'n wouldn't hurt nothing," Rawley said.

"I'll hold your position till you get back," Tim offered.

"Thanks," Rawley said. He wheeled his horse and galloped over to the buckboard where Nancy Hawkins sat. He dismounted and walked up to her. "Looks like we got a chance for another good-bye."

Nancy leaned down and kissed him. "I hope we don't have too many of these."

Rawley grinned and kissed her back. "If these good-byes is so good, I'll bet our hellos is gonna be jim-dandies!" He jumped back up in the saddle. "See you in a month, darling. I'll have greenbacks in my pockets and a hankering to get hitched with you."

"Don't you look at those Kansas girls," Nancy warned him.

"Sugar, they couldn't come close to matching my Texas rose," Rawley said.

Nancy smiled, and watched him ride back to the herd. She sat there for a moment, thinking of the man she loved as she watched him disappear with the others through the dusty haze raised by the herd that was now moving at a steady pace.

She brought herself out of her reverie. "I've got things to do!" Nancy picked up the reins and slapped them across the horse's back. The animal pulled against the weight of the buckboard and got it moving. As she headed back toward the ranch, she passed Myra Timmons, Darlene Dawson, and Penny Blevins, who had come out together to see their own men off.

Nancy waved to them. "It's a beautiful day, isn't it?"

"It sure is," Myra agreed.

"Don't forget we'll be over later today," Darlene reminded Nancy.

"That's right," Penny chimed in. "We've got a wedding to get ready for, don't we?"

"We sure do!" Nancy said happily. She continued on her way home. As she drove away, the last thing she could hear was Chaw Stevens' unmelodious voice fading in the distance as he sang:

"I got a ten-dollar horse and a forty-dollar saddle, and I'm heading up the trail for to punch Texas cattle. . . ."